RELICS OF MYSTICUS - BOOK ONE

The Serpent's Ring

H. B. BOLTON

For Brad, who encourages when others doubt,
For Lauren, who swims with mermaids,
For Wade, who believes in magic,
And for Cayce, who has probably
heard enough, but listens anyway,
This adventure is for you.

CONTENTS

Chapter One..Family Fun Day
Chapter Two...............................Hidden Treasure Found
Chapter Three.............................An Imp Is Not an It
Chapter Four................................A Model T Can't Fly
Chapter Five................................Sail Over Sand
Chapter Six..................................Tunnels in Trunks
Chapter Seven.......................Poppin-Droppin and Talkin'
Chapter Eight............................Trolls and Snow Globes
Chapter Nine.............................Cow Says: "Moo"
Chapter Ten...............................Binding Bronze
Chapter Eleven.........................Best-Kept Secret
Chapter Twelve.........................Sneaker Thief
Chapter Thirteen......................Frenzy of Fur
Chapter Fourteen.....................Stuck with Bull Sharks
Chapter Fifteen.........................Way of the Mermaid
Chapter Sixteen........................Wooden Shark-Pods
Chapter Seventeen...................Etched in Stone
Chapter Eighteen......................Travel by Turtle
Chapter Nineteen.....................Dripping in Diamonds
Chapter Twenty.......................Twirling and Flipping
Chapter Twenty-One...............Golden Whale-Pod
Chapter Twenty-Two...............Feisty Draugar
Chapter Twenty-Three.............Snapping Doorknob
Chapter Twenty-Four...............Faces in Waves
Chapter Twenty-Five................Feast and Folly
Chapter Twenty-Six..................Come Drown with Me
Chapter Twenty-Seven.............Not Again
Chapter Twenty-Eight...............Surf's Up, Dude
Chapter Twenty-Nine...............Fly Away Home
Chapter Thirty..........................Loop-the-Loops
Chapter Thirty-One.................Uninvited Guests
Magical Food Recipes:
        Poppin-Droppin, Woof-Out Bar, and Fizzy Whizzle
Index
        About the Author

CHAPTER ONE

FAMILY FUN DAY

GIANT WAVES APPROACHED—CLOSER, CLOSER. SEAWATER raced over shells and tiny crabs; sea foam nestled around Evan's toes.

"Surf's up," grinned Evan, clutching his surfboard. "I can do this."

Brilliant colors came to life within enormous sheets of water. Sparks of yellows, oranges, and reds formed into sinister shapes. They circled, edging closer.

Bull sharks!

Slowly, Evan's feet sank into the gritty, wet sand, and fear coursed throughout his fourteen-year-old body. He tightened his grip on the surfboard and tried to free his legs from the gluelike sand.

A large wave froze a few feet before him; colorful sharks circled inside.

"Get away!" Evan screamed at the swarming collection of teeth and coal-black eyes.

Something shoved against his shoulder! It pushed him into the wild surf. A trace of seawater splattered across his face; salt scorched his lips.

"Stop!" he yelled with all of his remaining strength.

Thrashing desperately, Evan sought to keep himself

from entering the wave.

The board!

Evan pulled it to him and landed with a painful thud onto a strangely hard surface.

◦◦◦◦◦

"Let go of me, pea brain. It's time to get up," Claire said as she yanked her arm from her brother's unexpected grip. "Remember, today is 'Family Fun Day.' Be late, and Mom and Dad will have a fit."

Evan's older sister swiftly exited his bedroom, most likely heading for the bathroom, where she would endlessly brush her hair and put all sorts of strange stuff on her face. No doubt, she will stink up the entire upstairs by slathering on flowery perfume. He was pretty sure he would have to use the downstairs bathroom.

"Wow, what a weird dream," said Evan, scratching the side of his head. He lifted his body off the wooden floor, and after shuffling through mounds of fallen clothes, he managed to locate something to wear. Sure, the outfit didn't exactly match, but his day was about to be spent in Boredomville anyway. His T-shirt probably had a stain on it somewhere; he didn't care. And there sat his lucky baseball cap. Now *that* he cared about. After all, he wore it to all of the University of Michigan games.

"Come on guys; let's go! We have lots to see!" His mom's voice echoed throughout the house.

"She sounds a little too enthusiastic," said Evan after meeting his sister at the top of the stairs. "If it were up to me, we'd be at the beach surfing the waves."

"Evan, you've lived in Michigan your entire life. Have you ever surfed on lake ripples? Get a clue," said Claire, wandering toward their parents.

"Whatever," he mumbled, following his sister down the stairs.

Ride in minivan: boring. Family day: boring. Museum: boring. Evan's life: boring. What bad luck being held captive by his parents for an entire day. Ever since his Mom took that job at the art gallery, she decided to declare every single Saturday *Family Fun Day*. It might as well have been called, "Evan Has to Do Something He Really Doesn't Want to Do Day."

He would much rather spend his day slurping down soda and eating chips while playing Hungry on Xbox or reading Breaking Down. Ah, that would have been more like it. Instead, he was stuck sitting in the backseat of the minivan, next to his annoying older sister.

"What are you looking at?" Claire scowled at him.

"I was just wondering how our parents managed to switch you at birth and keep it from you all these years," Evan teased.

"Kids, remember the rules; there's no fighting on *Family Fun Day*," said Mom, turning to face them. "Come on, you two. Can you please at least try to act civil to each other for just one day of the week?"

"It's kind of hard when he smells like a sweaty sock," Claire said with a smirk, clearly pleased with her witty comment.

"Oh yeah, well—" Evan started, but was cut short by his mom.

"Claire. Evan. I'm not kidding around here. We are going to spend time together as a family, even if it means sitting around the dining-room table and staring at each other all day!" The sharpness of their mother's tone contrasted with her normally cheerful demeanor. Evan and Claire looked at each other and nodded in a silent truce.

"All right, Mom; I'm sure we'll have a great day," said Claire, nudging into Evan.

"Yeah, it'll be fun," he said, trying to mimic his sister's false enthusiasm.

Immediately, their dad chimed, "You two will be surprised by how awesome Henry Ford's museum is. There will be old trains and planes. And that's just inside the building. Outdoors is a whole other world. People refer to it as Henry Ford's train set. That's because he brought in historical buildings from all around the world.

"Imagine a house being taken apart, brick by brick, board by board. It's then transported over sea by boat or across country by train. And then it arrives in many pieces and workers put it back together. It's really fascinating ..."

Blah, Blah, Blah.

Evan tried to keep a smile on his face, but he only paid attention to every other word. He did perk up when he heard Dad mention something about an exhibition of swords. And Dad should know; after all, he was a popular history teacher who was prone to being a little overly enthusiastic.

Last week, Evan's family spent an entire day at an art museum. It was all right, except for his father rambling on and on saying, '*Blah-blah*'s use of symmetry and *Blah-blah*'s use of color.' And since Mom sold artwork for a living, she too would pipe in details about every single sculpture, painting, drawing, lithograph, photograph, and tapestry. Honestly, she was even worse than Dad.

"Look, there's the building," said Dad, pointing off to his left. "It's truly amazing. I know I've said this a million times before, but you won't believe what's in there." He then continued to blather about the neat stuff contained inside each gallery.

When Dad turned into the parking lot, Evan was actually impressed by what he saw. A gigantic stone building was up ahead, and to his right was the entrance to Greenfield Village. Secretly, he allowed himself to join in his dad's excitement just a little. And from what Evan could see on this side of the high wall, he believed what his father had said about a whole other world was waiting on the other side.

While kicking at some small rocks, Evan followed the rest of his group through the main gates. He smiled as pebbles and sand scratched under his sneakers and tumbled along the sidewalk.

"Over there is the old Firestone Farm; we'll see it later. For now, I have arranged a surprise for you," said Dad, pointing in the direction of a small, gray building. "Our chariot awaits."

A sign reading "Happy Honking" hung down over the wooden deck. Evan practically jumped out of his skin when he heard an obnoxious honk-honk! A friendly enough looking man, wearing a goofy hat and red bowtie, drove a black Model T car in their direction.

"You folks ready for the tour?" asked the man with a large smile.

"You bet we are," Dad exclaimed. "That's right the Jones family is going to see Greenfield Village in style."

Evan's parents slid onto the back seat, and Claire jumped in between them. Evan quickly realized that he was left with the front seat, next to the newly dubbed Mr. Big Smile.

"Well, at least it's a convertible," mumbled Evan, slouching onto the old leather.

Welcome to Main Street. Is this your first time here?" Mr. Big Smile asked.

"We old folks have been here many times, but this is a first for our kids," said Mom over the engine.

"So, leave nothing out. We want to see and hear it all," said Dad, and with that, their lives would never be the same again.

CHAPTER TWO

HIDDEN TREASURE FOUND

THE GROUP PASSED BY MANY historical buildings, and Evan planted his chin on top of his balled-up hand. As far as tours went, it wasn't as boring as he had assumed. The tour guide sure did know his stuff.

The Model T rolled along, eventually slowing in front of a building marked "Closed for Renovation." Evan noticed something scamper below the roof's eaves. He could have sworn whatever he saw had a monkey's tail, but that would be impossible unless there was a petting zoo nearby. No matter what that thing was, it looked really weird.

"Did you see that?" Evan asked.

"You mean the house? Why, that was Dr. Irving's residence. It sat empty for more than eighty years before Greenfield Village purchased it. There were so many items to categorize that it took the team longer than normal to transport the house and its contents here. The house came all the way from England. But, I'm afraid it won't be open to the public for a few more weeks," said Mr. Big Smile, and he continued to drive idly down the single-lane road.

"Funny story with that house: I've heard the professor

10

went missing while out doing research. You see, he was a botanist, and from what I understand, he was brilliant. An amazing lab was hidden away inside the front study. It was only found when our team began preparing the house for the move."

Something shifted; there it was again! It stared right at Evan, a strange, little creature with bulging eyes.

"What is that?" Evan asked. But nobody paid any attention, and the creature disappeared. Now, Evan was eager for the tour to end. If Mr. Big Smile didn't hurry up, by the time Evan returned to Dr. Irving's house, the creature would be gone. Evan shifted in his seat and shuffled his feet, but the tour continued to drag.

"In another thirty minutes the clock will chime," said the driver as he parked the Model T. "You don't want to miss it. Something pretty unique happens at noon, and you kids will be in for a real surprise."

"We'll do that, thanks," Dad announced, leading the family down a pathway. "Your mother and I will reserve a spot on one of those park benches and wait for the clock. Would you two like to ride on the old-time carousel while we wait?"

"Actually, Dad, do you mind if I wander around for a little bit? I promise to come back in thirty minutes," Evan asked.

"Alrighty, but make it twenty-five. I'm telling you, the clock tower puts on a unique show. And afterward, we'll eat some ice cream," said Dad.

As Evan set off for Dr. Irving's home, he was still trying to make sense of that little thing he had seen. Evan walked past large trees and over lush grass. He kicked up dandelion seeds and breathed in the crisp summer air. And as he approached Dr. Irving's house, he felt like he had entered another time. It wasn't difficult to imagine what the house had looked like a hundred years ago.

Evan scanned along and under the roof's eaves—no sign of the creature. He wandered around to the back of the house—still nothing. He even crawled around to see underneath the house—just a bunch of dirt and cobwebs. He was about to leave when he saw three steps leading to the back porch. He sat down on the top step and sighed.

Just then, Evan was startled by the sounds of something like long toenails scurrying across a hard surface. He looked down the long porch in both directions, but nothing was there, nothing but an old rickety deck.

All of a sudden, that same sound came from inside the house. Evan jumped up and tried to peek through the dirt-covered windows. He stretched his shirt bottom and rubbed an area clean.

Inside, he could just about make out an old fashioned kitchen. He went to the door and tried the handle, certain it would be locked. But, to his amazement, it opened. Although it was against his better judgment, he went inside.

Floorboards squeaked and cobwebs were clustered in corners. Evan knew he should leave, but his curiosity got the better of him. He just couldn't stop his feet from traveling down the dark hallway. He wandered into the front study. A brick fireplace still held the odor of burnt logs. Wooden shelves lined every wall and were loaded with books.

Evan ran his finger across old leather spines. He laughed a little at how silly some of the names were: *Paint Your Roses Red, Edelweiss and Me, World of Mushrooms and Fungi, The Toadstool Diaries, Daffodils Unseen,* and *Exotic Plants Unleashed*, to name but a few. Evan spied a book on sea serpents and, intrigued, reached for its weathered binding. Inside, colorful illustrations depicted serpents in every possible size, shape, and color. A passage, hand-written in ink, stretched across a page:

12

Beware of the serpent, big and foul.
If unleashed, he'll loudly howl.
To his evil delight, water will surge,
And man will be washed away.

"That doesn't even rhyme," Evan mocked. "Dr. Irving may have been smart, but he wasn't much of a poet."

Evan didn't pay attention to how the minutes ticked away as he looked through each page. Finally, after glancing at his watch, he realized he was going to be late. He pushed the book back into the empty space, but it got stuck. Reaching his hand into the recess, his cuff caught on a little lever. He tugged at his sleeve—there was a sharp click and the entire bookshelf slid back and rolled sideways.

What had just happened?

Edging closer, Evan peered into the small room. As soon as he stepped inside, he was overwhelmed by a cloud of dust.

"Whew!" He let out a breath of air, trying to dislodge gunk from his lungs.

Evan entered the arid space and searched for a light. Tattered fabric hung over a stained-glass window. He scooted around objects and then pulled down the musty fabric. Sunlight streamed in, and Evan had to adjust his eyes.

The room looked like a science lab, but not the sort you'd see in today's classrooms. There were old-time objects everywhere: a gas lantern, wooden globes, bronze sculptures, a quill with parchment, and dried flowers. In fact, there were flowers and plants everywhere: inside glass vials, pinned to corkboards, and strewn across every available surface. A chalkboard, covered by white text and diagrams, sat next to a wooden desk.

Evan stared at the powdery letters and drawings of

13

plant life and marveled. "That must have been the last thing Dr. Irving worked on."

He tried to make sense of some of the rough sketches and ran his finger around a drawing of a serpent biting its own tail. This particular image stuck out like a sore thumb. What was it doing on a chalkboard covered with plants? Evan narrowed his eyes and tilted his head. The image directed his attention toward a collection of framed illustrations, hanging on the opposite wall. His curiosity led him to wander over in that direction.

Each frame contained an illustration that must have been torn out of a book. One of the pictures hung a little crooked, and as Evan tried to see better, he stretched up to his toes and bounced higher. He climbed onto a table and leaned in, further studying the details of the drawing.

The table wobbled, and he lost his balance. Just before hitting the floor, he managed to grab the picture and take it down. After missing a ceramic vase, he got back to his feet, all while still cradling the picture to his chest.

"That's strange," whispered Evan, running his hand over splinters along the back of the wooden frame.

He turned it over and stared. Attached to the back was a flat box. Evan slid it out of the shallow niche. Gold sparkled in the darkness. It was a ring in the shape of a serpent chewing on its own tail. He ran his finger over the tiny engravings along its skin and the two gems placed in its eyes. One was sapphire blue while the other was ruby red.

"What is this?" he wondered aloud.

"What are you doing in here?" shrilled a female voice from the doorway. Evan nearly jumped out of his skin. "You are going to be in sooo much trouble when Mom and Dad find out! You aren't supposed to be in here. Didn't you read the sign that said 'Restricted Area'?"

Evan turned to face his sister and glared. She had

scared him half to death, and he needed a moment to muster something clever to say.

"Let's go," instructed Claire. "Now!" Her arms crossed sternly over her chest and her foot made an annoying tapping sound.

"Wait a minute. Have you ever seen anything so cool in your life? Just look at this," he said, sliding his hand through the ring. It was too large to be a bracelet and too small to be worn as a necklace; so, he placed the band around his forearm.

"Claire, the jewels on this ring are starting to glow. Way cool!"

"Come on, let's get out of here," said Claire, stalking over to Evan. But as she grabbed him, an electric bolt surged and passed between them. The entire room gave off a blinding white light. Its current threw Claire against a bookshelf and she fell to the floor, bombarded by tumbling objects. Evan rushed to her aid and, by pushing aside scattered fragments, managed to reach her.

"Claire, are you all right?"

"Help me up," she said, reaching for him.

Evan extended his hand, but as he looked down toward his sister, he realized the golden serpent was still wrapped around his arm. He leaned back, missing Claire completely.

"Hello, I'm right here!" she exclaimed.

"I know, sorry," said Evan, staring at the brilliant light coming from inside the serpent's bejeweled eyes.

"What is that?" she asked before grabbing it. "Do you think this is real gold?" She slid the circular object over her wrist and up her arm, admiring it from every angle.

"I thought you said we needed to leave. You should probably give that to me," said Evan, snatching it back.

"I know. It's just ... have you ever seen anything so beautiful?" she said dreamily.

All of a sudden, a loud scratching noise came from

outside the secret room. It was followed by the slamming of a door.

"It must be a security guard," Claire whispered tensely. "We're not supposed to be in here."

"Hurry up! We need to make tracks!"

The two rushed out of the house, but as soon as they stepped onto the front porch, they froze. Something was wrong, terribly wrong. Nothing was as it should have been. The sky was orange, the ground was covered with a pale-blue mist, and there were long, colorful tubes weaving around pink clouds.

"Evan, what's going on here?" Claire asked, staring wide-eyed at the glasslike cluster of trees.

"I have no idea. Maybe, we should go back inside the house."

"No, we need to find Dad and Mom. They have to be here somewhere," said Claire, grabbing Evan's arm.

"Look, over there." He pointed to a purple bench. "Is it glass?"

"It looks like it," said Claire. She then turned and stared at Evan.

"What?" he finally asked.

"The bracelet, it's still on your arm."

"Oh man. That's just great! Now we're going to get in trouble for stealing!"

"Evan, I think that's the least of our problems. How are we supposed to find Mom and Dad?"

"I'm not sure."

"Why did you have to go into that house in the first place?" Claire yelled, pacing back and forth.

"I thought there was a monkey under the roof. I had to go back to see if I was imagining things."

"Well, of course you were imagining things. You usually are."

"You have to admit, all that stuff was pretty cool. Can you believe the secret room?"

"Evan, what I can't believe is what's circling up there!"

16

CHAPTER THREE

AN IMP IS NOT AN IT

ALOUD SHRIEK CAME FROM RIGHT overhead. Evan ducked and threw his arms protectively over his head. He felt a strong tug on the bracelet and then landed back with a thud. Looking upward, he spied a large tropical bird. It had ridiculously long wings with blinding feathers, each one coated in brilliant shades of green and blue with flecks of gold. Evan watched as it flew away—its talons clutching the golden ring.

"No, no, no, no, no! Not the Serpent's Ring, not the Serpent's Ring!" erupted a strange gurgling voice. Evan searched for whatever made that horrible noise, but all he saw was a puffy, lavender cloud.

"Aahh!" Claire screamed. "What ... what is that?"

Evan looked again; this time, he saw a green and black creature scurrying around, kicking up small gems.

"This is bad, very, very bad. Oh dear, oh dear," said the little creature, its hands tugging at its tiny green mohawk of hair.

"Evan, Evan, um, do you see that?" Claire muttered.

"I'm not sure," Evan answered.

"I am not a 'that,' nor am I an 'it.' I am an imp!" said the creature. "You may call me Dunkle."

17

"Hey, you're that thing I saw at Dr. Irving's house," said Evan.

"Excuse me, as I explained previously, I am not a thing. I am an imp! And you are being quite rude, even for a human."

At last, the imp held still long enough for Evan to examine him. One word came to mind: pee-yew. Dunkle stood at around 21 inches, but he produced a stench that should have come from a 21-foot ogre. Evan tried to place the odor; it wasn't a heap of decayed garbage nor that of a spoiled fish. Truth be told, it smelled like rotten cheese.

The imp had skin resembling a dart frog—mostly green with a pattern of black rings and swirls covering the parts of his body that was exposed (which was most of him). A very small portion of the imp was covered by a brown vest. Resting on his chest was a necklace of a serpent carved into the smooth golden stone. Exaggerated ears pointed straight out from the imp's head. In fact, everything about him was exaggerated in some way or another. His belly was portly, and his head, hands, and feet were far too large for his spindly body. Plus, he had a lengthy whiplike tail.

"How long are you going to stare at me? Come on, come on, let us get over the initial shock and move forward. We are in serious trouble here. Do you realize what you have just done?" exclaimed Dunkle, his huge hands still waving above his head.

"No, I have no idea what on Earth you are talking about. Would you mind filling me in?" Evan asked, feeling a mixture of frustration and fear. He glanced over at his sister. She hadn't moved much since Dunkle's arrival. It was kind of strange to see her motionless—cool, but strange.

"That's just it. We aren't exactly on Earth anymore. Haven't you noticed the sky is tangerine?"

"Of course I have," said Evan.

"Well, the golden ring you found in Dr. Irving's lab opened a portal to Sagaas, Land of the Gods."

"Land of the Gods?" Evan repeated.

"Yes. Gods and creatures in many ancient myths are real and thriving. Just because you cannot see them does not mean they are not very real."

"But I don't see any gods or creatures," said Evan. "Where are they?"

"Each myth exists in its own realm. Sagaas is what you might consider a station of sorts—a connection to all of the realms."

"I still don't understand why we're the only ones here. I mean, you're here, so where are all of the other mythical creatures? You know, like giants and dragons?"

"My dear child, we are the only ones here because the gods do not like to leave their own realm."

"All right, so how can we travel to one of the realms?" asked Evan. "I'd like to see a dragon."

"Sagaas is very similar to your airports and train stations. We shall follow the signs leading to Asgard and only Asgard."

"Um, no offense, but I don't see any signs."

"Do you see the sculpture over there, the one with a bird-god holding a rare jewel toward the sky?" asked Dunkle, pointing off to his left.

"Sure."

"That is a replication of the Golden Staff of Ra. If you wanted to travel to the realm of Egyptian mythology, you would follow that symbol and the orange mist."

"Cool," said Evan.

"What about Atlantis?" Claire asked, awakening from her trancelike state.

"Of course there is a portal for Atlantis, but we need to focus on the Serpent's Ring and lavender mist," said Dunkle. "Ah, there it is."

Evan looked over to where the imp was pointing his long, gangly arm. A glass replica of the Serpent's Ring towered above the colorful trees. Lavender mist circled its base and continued in a straight line toward the east.

"Dunkle, what's the big deal with the Serpent's Ring?" asked Evan. "Why is it so important we get it back?"

"The Serpent's Ring might be just one relic from the great Mysticus Orb, but it still contains enough power to destroy all of Terra. If it were to fall into the wrong hands, the consequences could be catastrophic."

"What's Terra?" Evan asked.

"Why, your Earth, of course."

The fresh breeze cut right through Evan's skin. He could barely move, but he managed to mumble, "Did it just fall into the wrong hands?"

"I am afraid so. The bird that stole the Serpent's Ring is one of Aegir's soldiers. Which means the Serpent's Ring is on its way to the Norse sea god."

"Wait, who's Aegir?" Evan asked.

"Clearly, you have not studied Norse mythology, have you?" Dunkle stated rhetorically.

"Sure, a little. There's the god Thor and Odin and some trolls with big noses or something," said Claire.

"Oh yeah, and Loki," interrupted Evan. "I like him; he's funny."

"My dear children, there are many, many gods and goddesses from Norse mythology," said Dunkle irritably. "Aegir is the god of the sea. He has always been, shall I say, different. But after the most recent oil spill in one of his precious coral reefs, he is completely incensed. He wants to flood the entire planet and can use the Serpent's Ring to do just that."

"But why would he want to wipe out everybody on Earth—I mean Terra?" Evan asked nervously.

"Aegir believes, by washing away mankind, he will be able to revitalize the world," said Dunkle. "In some ways,

I agree with him. But I think there must be another way to deal with mankind."

Evan barely flinched, barely breathed. In fact, he was barely able to comprehend all he had just heard. "Let me get this straight; what you're telling us is that an angry sea god is trying to flood the entire planet?" Evan asked, and the imp nodded his head.

"How is the Serpent's Ring supposed to help him with that?"

"Do you remember the shape of the Serpent's Ring?" Dunkle asked.

"Yes, it was a serpent, circling to bite its tail," Claire chimed.

"Right, right—only imagine a serpent so big, it's able to wrap its body around the entire world. Now, that serpent would be Jormundgand," Dunkle said slowly, emphasizing the last word. "Now, if Jormundgand lets go of his tail, then Terra, as we know it, will be flooded and destroyed. The Serpent's Ring can be used as a key to unlock the giant sea serpent."

"Slow down there. I don't want any part of sea gods and giant serpents," exclaimed Evan.

But Dunkle didn't seem to hear Evan, or perhaps the imp didn't care about what the boy had to say. Instead of listening, he stroked his chin thoughtfully. "Let me see; we need to fly over to Lake Huron and sail through the lavender tunnel leading into Asgard."

"How do you suggest we fly to Lake Huron, and how are we going to sail to this Asgard place?" Claire asked.

Dunkle didn't acknowledge her, he was too distracted. "That'll do. Right over there, right over there." Dunkle pointed his long, boney finger toward the Model T car.

"Are you crazy? We can't take that car!" Evan exploded, pacing back and forth. "Besides, what is a Model T doing here? Nothing else around this place looks the same."

"Certainly, most objects from your world disappear

21

when you enter Sagaas. Sometimes, however, a few manmade items manage to sneak in. That Model T must have a very interesting past, indeed."

"I can drive it," Claire stated.

"Not likely," said Evan.

"Hey, I'm sixteen and passed my driving test. All I have to do is figure out the gears," said Claire, walking toward the old automobile.

Just then, Dunkle leapt in front of her, and she teetered backward. "What are you doing?" yelled Claire.

"No need to drive, no need to drive. Get in, get in. I'll explain," said Dunkle. He then shook his head. "Terrific. Here, I have spent a century perfecting my speech, and because of you, I have reverted back to my impish way of speaking."

Evan reluctantly followed his sister and Dunkle to the car. Claire sat on the backseat, and Evan joined her—anything to get away from that cheesy odor coming from the imp.

Dunkle climbed behind the wheel, and turned around. "So, which one of you can make this car fly?"

CHAPTER FOUR

A MODEL T CAN'T FLY

C LAIRE AND EVAN PEERED OVER at each other and scrunched up their eyebrows in bewilderment.

"Clearly the imp is off his rocker," Evan whispered, and Claire giggled.

"You two must pay attention. When you put on the Serpent's Ring, did you notice anything strange?" Dunkle asked, studying the two passengers.

Claire said excitedly, "Yeah, it shocked me and made the room light up."

"That's not all it did," said Dunkle. "I am afraid not only did you open a portal to Sagaas, your DNA was slightly altered."

"How do you mean, altered?" Evan asked. "Don't tell me we're going to turn into mad-raving imps."

"Not likely, I am sorry to say," Dunkle quipped. "Both of you were given a power. Now, I am wondering, which one of you can move this car?"

Evan and Claire shrugged their shoulders. Evan leaned back, put his arms across his chest, and grumbled, "This is ridiculous."

"How can we find out?" Claire asked, sounding sincerely interested.

23

"Concentrate," said the imp. "First, concentrate on moving the wheels. Think about them and imagine they are rolling forward."

Claire squint her eyes and pursed her lips. After a minute of fierce concentration, a rush of air released through her mouth, and she collapsed against the backseat.

Evan laughed. "Seriously, you are as loony as the imp."

"At least, I'm trying to do something here! What about you? Aren't you going to try?" Claire bellowed.

"No," said Evan flatly.

"Evan, an enormous bird swooped down and stole the Serpent's Ring from your arm. We are in a Model T with an imp, and the sky is tangerine with rainbow-colored clouds. Humor me, and try to move this blasted car with your mind!" said Claire, grabbing Evan's shirt collar. "If you don't, I will make your life miserable. Got it?"

Evan looked at Dunkle, then back at his sister before saying, "Fine, I'll do it. But, just for the record, this is bizarre."

Dunkle gave him a little smile, and Evan brought in a large breath of air. He imagined the tires turning, but nothing happened.

"See, I told you. This is ridiculous," he sighed.

"No, try again," encouraged Dunkle.

Evan rolled his eyes and then concentrated. Suddenly, the Model T swayed and a lavender mist billowed out from underneath the car.

"Whoa, what happened?" said Evan, his eyes wide.

"You, my boy, are telekinetic," said Dunkle with obvious delight.

"Come on, Evan, try it again," Claire encouraged.

"You can do this. Just imagine the wheels turning," instructed Dunkle.

Evan looked back and forth between Claire and

Dunkle. After careful deliberation, he decided to risk looking like a fool and try it again. He closed his eyes and imagined his hand was pushing the tires around and around. Suddenly, he felt the car rock and heard his sister gasp. He opened his eyes. Not only did the tires roll, the entire flippin' car was floating!

"Argh!" Evan shouted, and with that, the car fell back down, producing a startling jolt.

"Ouch!" Claire yelped and swatted at her brother. "Why did you drop us?"

"Am I the only one here who finds it the tiniest bit odd that we were flying in a Model T?" shouted Evan.

Claire placed her hand gently on his shoulder. "Evan, yes, it is strange. But if we don't get over it, then according to Dunkle, everything we care about will soon be covered in water. I'm not any happier than you are, but I'm trying to deal with it and so should you."

Evan took another second to collect himself before sitting upright and taking hold of the front seat. "I think this will work better if I'm behind the wheel," he said, jumping over. He looked at Dunkle, who nodded slightly.

"Ready?" Dunkle asked.

"As I'll ever be," said Evan, his bare white knuckles clutching the wheel.

Again, he filled his lungs with air and concentrated. To his surprise, the car lifted and hovered in place.

"Now, forward," instructed Dunkle.

"Wicked," said Evan as air blew through his hair and whispered into his ears.

"Be very careful; you must continue to concentrate and don't look down," said Dunkle.

Evan hadn't considered looking down. But now that Dunkle mentioned it, he just couldn't resist. Evan peeked over the car door, and the Model T fell!

"Concentrate! Don't lose your focus!" shouted Claire.

The car froze in place. Evan tried not to peek over the

side, as they were floating really high. The wind kicked up, and Dunkle clamped together his tiny brown vest, shielding his reptilianlike skin.

"Um, Dunkle, this is sort of intense. I'm trying to keep calm. Which direction should I steer the car?" Evan inquired, guiding the car between interwoven glass tunnels.

Dunkle stretched his mangled-looking arm eastward. "Fly this car in a straight line, that way." Evan did as the imp instructed and carefully rotated their flying automobile. "You might want to go a little faster."

"Hold on, this might get dicey," Evan said and pushed their levitating car toward the Great Lake.

Evan felt as if he had stepped inside a brilliantly colored kaleidoscope. He shivered as he passed a few mist-laden gateways. Up ahead, a tropical-looking island rested on billowing clouds. Crystal columns stretched high above the fog. Enormous palm trees swayed back and forth, and a waterfall rushed down a high, glass rock formation and over the side of the cloud. Water droplets trickled down.

The imp shoved his arm in front of Evan's nose and said, "Aim north-east—that way."

"Do you mind moving your arm? Actually, if you could scoot far away—that's it, a little farther." Evan realized, however, that Dunkle didn't smell quite so bad now. He leaned toward the imp and sniffed. Odd, Dunkle smelled like a tree, a nicely scented pine.

"Don't look so surprised," began Dunkle. "I smell bad only when I am angry or upset or nervous. Normally, I smell like this. All imps take on the odor from the tree under which they were born." The imp must have been really happy, because the entire area smelled like a Christmas-tree lot.

"There, there! Put the car down on the sand," Dunkle said and closed his eyes. He then made a high piercing sound, forcing Evan and Claire to grab their ears. The imp swayed from side to side, continuing to screech for at least a minute. It was difficult to concentrate with that ear-perforating noise, but Evan managed to land safely.

"Please, don't ever do that again," Evan barked, sticking his finger in his ear, but he still couldn't stop the ringing.

"Evan, the sand looks like tiny pearls!" Claire shouted. "Dunkle, is it safe to touch?"

"Of course it's safe," said Dunkle, leaping over the car door.

Dunkle became a swift blur, his speed undeterminable. With a stick in hand, he tumbled over and across the shimmering sand, making scratches and pushing sand piles around here and there, little sparks flying up in the air. Evan and Claire watched in amusement. The little imp flipped and rolled around, splattering bits of pearlescent sand.

"There," said Dunkle, standing back to admire his work.

"What were you doing?" Claire asked.

"You will soon see," Dunkle sang.

"Dunkle, Dunkle!" a second gurgling voice came from some purple bushes.

"Barfel!" Dunkle squealed, scurrying over to meet the other imp. Not that Evan was very familiar with imps, but an imp is what it looked like. This imp's skin was different than Dunkle's. It was predominantly burnt-orange with darker brown splotches. He too had a bushy mohawk trailing over his head, but instead of being green, like Dunkle's, it was red.

The two imps spoke a language consisting of gulps and gurgles. Every so often, Dunkle would motion toward Evan and Claire. After awhile, the orange imp's face started to sag.

"The sound I made earlier was a call to my dear

friend, Barfel," explained Dunkle. "This is Barfel. And please pronounce it correctly, *BAR-fell*."

"Dunkle, why is he here?" Evan questioned. Then, he said quietly to Claire, "The last thing we need is another stinky imp." At which Claire chuckled.

"Ah-hum," Dunkle interrupted. "Barfel is going to help us. We will need all the friends we can get. And for the record, his personal aroma is from the tree under which he was born: cedar."

CHAPTER FIVE

SAIL OVER SAND

THE TWO IMPS SCAMPERED OVER and around the large drawing in the sand. Dunkle and Barfel discussed their sketch as if it were a great work of art. Both nodded their heads and made various modifications, and occasionally, Barfel would clap. They ran here and there, grabbing random objects and piling them up in the center of the sketch: driftwood, old rope, they even took Evan's prize baseball cap. After a minute of this, they turned toward Claire. Dunkle and Barfel made a few more garbled sounds and approached her.

"Make the boat, make the boat!" exclaimed Barfel, bouncing up and down.

"Dunkle is right. You do smell like cedar," said Evan.

"Ah-hem," sounded Dunkle. "Claire, your brother was not the only person in Dr. Irving's lab. If you recall, you were there, too. And the last time the Serpent's Ring was activated, there were two powers given. One was the power to move objects with the mind: Evan claimed that power. The other was the ability to manipulate matter."

"Really, I can manipulate matter? Please explain," said Claire.

"I believe the second power—transfiguration—was

29

given to you, Claire. You should be able to change an object's form from one thing to another," Dunkle answered.

"So, if I wanted to, I could turn my sandals into boots?" Claire asked, and Dunkle nodded.

"Try it, try it!" Barfel chimed. "Sandals into boots!"

"Please, just focus on making a boat," said Dunkle. "You two can play with fashion later."

"After all that has happened, I guess I'll believe anything," said Claire, sounding rather adult in her wisdom. "What do you suggest I do?"

"We need to travel to Asgard by boat," said Dunkle. "We must use the materials at hand. As you may or may not know, when heated, sand turns into glass. Imagine melting down sand and then molding it into a boat. Now, you will also need to stretch the fabric from Evan's cap into a sail, and use these old ropes to tether it. The drawing Barfel and I sketched can be used as a guide. Clearly, it is an outline of a ship."

"What about that stick, over there?" Evan asked.

"Leave it as is; we'll need it for firewood," said Dunkle.

"Go on, go on!" Barfel cheered, in a distracting sort of way.

For a second time, Claire looked at her brother. It appeared as if she were saying "Help me!" with her eyes. Evan didn't know how to help her, so he shrugged his shoulders and motioned toward the imps' sketch.

"All right, if Evan can fly a car, I can make a boat. I'll need some serious therapy after all of this," whispered Claire as she approached the imps' drawing. "Oh, now I see it. It's a rough outline of a ship. Okay, here goes nothing."

She stared down, and suddenly, Evan felt a slight tremor beneath his sneakers. The sand shifted, and in a giant swoop, tiny grains flew into the air. A thick cloud swirled and whirled. From the beach, a mound of pearlescent sand began to take form. Claire's arms slowly rose and fell, like those of a music conductor, and with each fluid movement, grains of sand molded into the walls of a ship: a Viking ship.

Another blast of sand and a dragon formed into the bow. Its scales etched along the ship's sides. A mast shot up, and once extended, unrolled into a sail that stretched the ship's width. The canvas was navy blue, and an image of Jormundgand, the sea serpent, was stitched with the yellow thread from the "M" off Evan's hat.

"Too cool!" Evan gaped at the marvel arising. "But in all due respect, it doesn't feel right to have the M from my hat turned into a serpent. The least you could do is change the serpent into a giant M, for Michigan."

"For the first time, Little Brother, I'll have to agree with you," said Claire. She wove her hand through the air as if she were writing with a pencil. The threading from the serpent unraveled and was replaced swiftly by an enormous yellow M.

"Much better," said Evan.

Claire sank to the ground and tossed her hair forward. She knelt down with her arms slumped, gasping for air. This was typical behavior for Evan's sister, who always was a bit dramatic. He wondered how long she would remain in her bowed position. Another second passed, and Evan gave her a round of applause.

"Great job, Sis!" Evan cheered. "Encore, encore!"

"Funny, Evan," said Claire, and after lifting her head, she sat back to admire her work. "Whoa."

"Very nicely done," said Dunkle. "Remember, you can change only the *form* of an object. You will not be able to change wood into metal. Wood stays wood. You can only mold it into another shape. Understand?"

"I think so," said Claire, but she didn't really sound very certain.

The imps circled the outside of the glass ship, tapping along its bow and stern. They both scuttled onto the vessel, making scratching sounds as they scampered.

"All teasing aside, it's really cool. I like the fact you made it a Viking ship. Nice," said Evan, placing his hand on Claire's shoulder.

"Who knew, right?" said Claire.

The vessel was practically invisible, as it was totally clear. Evan knocked on its side and was shocked to feel its strength. He looked up the high glass wall.

"How are we supposed to climb up there?" said Evan, still appraising Claire's handiwork.

A few feet away, sand started to shift. Up from a small cloud, a thin string of melted glass appeared. It wove and danced in the air, forming into a set of stairs. It coiled around a few times before stretching up to the side of the ship.

Evan looked over at his sister and stared in wonderment. "Impressive," he said before ascending.

Slowly, she lifted herself and followed him.

"This is the most awesome thing I've ever seen!" declared Evan, running across the deck. After slipping a little, he added, "And slick."

They would travel in style, no denying it. As Evan's excitement heightened, he almost forgot they were going to face a giant sea serpent and an angry sea god.

"Now what?" Claire asked Dunkle. "I mean, how exactly are we going to move this ship into the lake?"

Dunkle looked at Evan.

"I've got this one, Sis. Just leave it to me," said Evan brashly. He strode over to the ship's bow and looked down. They were still on land, quite far from the water. "I know I can do this."

After taking in a deep breath, he imagined edging forward. And just like that, the ship moved. First, it sliced over sand, making a deep impression behind, and then tiny waves started to lap its bow. Before long, their ship cut through the yellow-orange water, moving rather swiftly.

"We can see through the ship's bottom," Evan exclaimed. "Whoa, Claire, the water's orange."

"It's beautiful. Dunkle, why is the water orange?" Claire asked.

"The water is clear," Dunkle explained. "The ground underneath is fluorescent and its color shines up to the surface."

"Cool," said Evan before looking up. "Which way are we heading?"

"Set our course north. We still need to slip through the lavender tunnel, leading us to Asgard," said Dunkle.

"Tunnel?" said Claire. "I thought we were going to sail through a puff of mist. What sort of tunnel are you talking about?"

"A tunnel made of glass," said Dunkle. "The tunnel is harmless; I can assure you of that."

"Just call me Captain Evan," said Evan, rushing back. "All I need now is my cap."

Claire knelt down, and to Evan's amazement, slid her hand right through the deck as if it were soft butter. Then, she molded the doughlike blob into a Viking helmet.

"Way cool," Evan announced. "But that's not going to work for me."

Barfel snapped, "I'll wear it! I'll wear it!"

Claire smiled and then waved her hand. Blue stitching unraveled from the sail. It floated in front of Evan and was woven miraculously into a pirate hat.

"You made me a pirate hat? Claire, I'm fourteen not seven."

"Evan, I'm through with hat-making. We need to move on to more important things—like saving the world."

"Well, I guess it'll work," Evan said before placing the

hat upon his head.

He leaned back, hand on rudder, and guided the ship north. The voyage was smooth and easy. Other than the strange tangerine haze, the day was perfect. It had been a long time since his family sailed on Lake Huron. Why couldn't Family Fun Day include more time on a boat?

Evan turned to see how far they were from shore. "Goodbye," he said, as the shoreline disappeared from view.

Up ahead, Evan saw a lavender mist. He sat upright and paid close attention. It was a good thing too, since he almost rammed the boat into a purple object that was rising up out of the sea. It rose higher and higher, and as soon as the dragonlike head surfaced, Evan realized it was the statue of the Serpent's Ring.

The air around the Viking ship became dense and deepened to a darker violet. A light began to glow from deep inside the heart of the large replica of the Serpent's Ring, and Evan had to shield his eyes. Water rolled, making it difficult for him to steer. The boat rocked from side to side and was tossed forward like a cannonball.

"I take it, this is where the tunnel is," Evan hollered.

The imps didn't respond; they were too busy laughing. Evan looked at Claire, whose face was an interesting shade of green.

"Are there any life preservers on this thing?" she hollered above the thundering claps.

"I think you forgot to make them," teased Evan.

Again, their boat was thrown! This time, it soared through the air before being pulled into a large glass tube. They raced faster and faster through the lavender tunnel until they stopped abruptly. The tube had opened up into a circular area with five more tubes splitting off into different directions.

"Dunkle, what are we supposed to do now?" Evan shouted.

"Steer the ship toward the one on the far right," said Dunkle.

"Why that one?" Claire asked.

"Because that one will take us to see Dr. Irving," Dunkle said quite matter-of-factly.

"Dr. Irving's still alive? Does he live in Asgard?" Evan asked.

"Where else would he be?" Dunkle quipped. "After marrying the goddess Vor, he certainly couldn't return to your world. Gods and goddesses are not allowed there."

"He married a goddess?" said Claire, throwing her hands in the air. "Why am I not surprised?"

"Who's Vor?" Evan asked.

"Vor is the goddess who knows everything about everything," said Dunkle. "She will know exactly what to do."

Suddenly, orange water surged up and tossed the boat forward. Quickly, Evan turned the rudder, and the ship practically flew into the far-right tunnel. After swirling around a few more loops, the ship shot out of the tunnel, landing safely on the water's surface and sliding the length of a football field right up to the shore. Evan stared at his sister. She raised her head and looked around.

Dunkle hopped along the deck, cheering, "We have arrived! What an invigorating ride!"

"Land ho, land ho!" Barfel announced from the top of the mast. He then swung down the pole. "Land ho, land ho!" he sang and did a silly little dance, his red mohawk swaying to and fro.

"Welcome to Asgard," said Dunkle, a smile consuming his entire face. "I am home."

Evan scanned Asgard's shoreline. The ocean was now a nice familiar blue. Enormous mountains jutted into the cloudless turquoise sky, their high peaks covered with snow. Leafy green trees concealed rolling hills. Teeny flecks sparkled and zipped from place to place—resting here, then whizzing there.

Evan scooped up a handful of sparkling sand and allowed it to stream through his fingers. "Is this gold?"

"Yes. Gold dust it is, it is," said Barfel.

"It will not do you any good here, other than making golden sand castles with it. Let us go. We have quite a ways to walk," Dunkle explained and headed toward the woods.

"Evan, you might want to lose the hat," Claire said. "I mean, you'll look kind of silly wearing a pirate hat in front of the professor."

Evan agreed and threw the hat on board the ship.

Dunkle skipped across the sparkling sand and then dove into a patch of tall wavy grass. A breeze whipped through the blades, strumming enchanting music as they swayed. Dunkle led them into a wooded area. Vibrant leaves drifted from branches, covering their path.

Dunkle stopped abruptly in his tracks and then rushed over to a large tree. He ran his hand up and along lines in the bark, his fingernails scratched between its grooves. Evan and Claire waited with Barfel and watched curiously.

"I believe this is the correct tree," said Dunkle. "But I had better double check. We would not want to end up at the wrong door." Dunkle looked down and searched the ground. He spied a rock that looked a lot like a bowling ball. Dunkle hurried over to it. He then rotated his hand above the moss-covered rock and chanted something in another language. Dirt rumbled, as the rock shifted from side to side. It rose from the ground, higher and higher, until it reached the same height as Dunkle, which was only around two feet. Slowly, an area opened. Sand sprayed out as it gagged and sputtered. And then it lifted its eyelids. The rock had a face!

"Ah, Dunkle, it is good to see you again," said the

rock.

"Gynge, it has been ages," Dunkle exclaimed. "How have you been, old chap?"

"Other than this mess of moss growing down into my eyes, I have been well," said the rock. "You must be here to see the professor. He will be pleased you have returned."

"How is the old fellow? It has been awhile since I last saw him," said Dunkle.

"Too, long," said the rock, more animation in his expression than before. "Just because you guard the ... are uh, on a secret mission, does not mean you cannot visit more often."

"Gynge, my comrades here know about the Serpent's Ring," said Dunkle. He then gave a brief introduction between Evan, Claire, Barfel, and the rock. "That is why we have come. The Serpent's Ring has been stolen by Aegir."

"Great Odin! What will you do? How will you manage to retrieve it?" asked Gynge.

"You can see why it is imperative we speak with the professor," said Dunkle.

"Of course, of course," said Gynge. "I shall allow you passage."

"Thank you," said Dunkle.

"Good luck to you," said Gynge before spinning around a few times. From a short distance away, Evan heard wood snap and split.

CHAPTER SIX

TUNNELS IN TRUNKS

A SMALL OPENING MATERIALIZED IN THE base of a nearby tree. Dunkle ran over, hollering, "Follow me," and he disappeared through the opening. Before long, the hole had grown, stretching to Evan's height.

"This way! This way!" Barfel shouted and bounced over, before rushing through.

"I'm not going in there," Claire said with a tremor in her voice.

"Come on, Claire. I'll be right behind you," Evan reassured her.

Inside the tree, the four travelers descended down a stairwell made of intricately intertwined roots. At the bottom, a larger cavern with passageways and tunnels wove and wound through a labyrinth of corridors.

"Unbelievable," said Claire in a hush.

"What is this place?" Evan asked, straining to see past the glow of Dunkle's fire-lit torch.

"Consider this Asgard's solution to underground travel," Dunkle explained.

"We're safe down here, safe down here—not up there," added Barfel.

"Except we have to walk," complained Evan. "I'm

getting tired. When do we take a break?"

"Not far now, not far now," cheered Barfel.

Evan and Claire followed Dunkle and Barfel through the long tunnel, illuminated by a warm golden glow. Occasionally, Dunkle allowed them to pause and admire something sculpted along the wooden walls: deer, bears, birds, and other creatures Evan didn't recognize. He ran his fingertips along the polished wood, fascinated by patterns in the grain.

At last, they reached a tall, narrow door. A serpent biting its tail was carved into the red wood. It was the very same image Evan had seen in Dr. Irving's lab: the Serpent's Ring. His insides quivered. How was he supposed to explain to Dr. Irving he didn't mean to take the Serpent's Ring? Now it was on its way to Aegir, and it was his fault.

The door creaked open, and a thin man with salt-and-pepper hair poked his head out to greet them. "I wondered when you would arrive," he said pleasantly and opened the door a little wider. "Come inside, please."

Evan hung his head and dragged his feet over the carved wooden threshold. He believed it was best to be as inconspicuous as possible. So he hid behind his sister. But after taking his first step onto the shiny black and white marble floor, he lifted his head a little. This place looked nothing like he expected.

"Where did you get all of this stuff?" Claire asked, running her hand over a red leather sofa. "No offense, but I can't imagine there's a modern furniture store right around the corner."

"No, no," said Dr. Irving in his educated sounding English accent. "The first thing you must remember while you are here is that not everything is as it seems. You will discover that *I* am a clever man and have my ways."

"It might also help that you are married to a *goddess*,

one who happens to have spectacular taste." A dark-haired woman with golden brown skin glided into the room. "You must be Claire and Evan. We have been expecting you."

"Expecting us? How could you possibly know we were coming?" Claire asked. Vor approached her and reached for her hand. The goddess flipped it over and stared at Claire's open palm.

"Darling girl, I know everything. I am Vor," said Vor with her musical accent. "Hmm, interesting; you have a very mysterious past."

Claire interjected, "I hardly think coming from the suburbs in Michigan makes for a mysterious past."

"Your soul runs deep; you have a very rich heritage," said Vor.

"I would hardly call us rich—comfortable, but definitely not rich," said Claire.

Vor smiled and released Claire's hand. The goddess turned to Evan, who was trying to blend into a wall. "And hiding over there, you must be Evan. Please, do not be afraid. I know what happened was, dare I say, a mishap?"

Nervously, Evan chewed on his lip while edging himself in her direction. He was uneasy and found it impossible to gaze into her all-knowing brown eyes.

"I'm so sorry. Believe me, I didn't mean to cause all of this trouble," said Evan, looking down at the silky red fabric of Vor's dress. It was draped around her body like Kool-Aid swirling in a glass. Her feet were bare, and he wondered if he should remove his sneakers.

"I do believe you," said Vor, placing her hand under his chin and lifting his head. "Now, we must sit and talk. There is much to discuss, and we have so little time."

"I will be just a moment with your refreshments," said Dr. Irving, dashing for the kitchen.

"Professor, please allow me to be of assistance,"

Dunkle exclaimed and leapt across the room. He then scuttled behind Dr. Irving, speaking in that strange language of his. To Evan's surprise, the professor nodded his head and used his hands to gesture in return. In fact, it looked as if he and Dunkle were having an intriguing conversation. Is it possible the professor actually understood the imp?

Dr. Irving opened a large chrome refrigerator and relieved it of some food. Dunkle was right beside him, helping carry the load over to the kitchen counter. Evan couldn't believe how flashy his surroundings were. The room consisted mostly of objects that were black and white, shiny chrome, and red. Glossy-white shelves held black, white, and red books. Instead of antique trinkets, like in the Professor's other house, everything here was shiny and clean. Large canvases with black, white, and red paint lined the walls. Stylish black-and-white photographs appeared here and there.

Mmmm. Aroma from fresh-baked goodies drifted toward Evan, and his mouth watered. He watched as Dr. Irving lined plates and various utensils on top of a glass platter. Evan realized he should listen more closely to Vor, but he couldn't stop keeping tabs on what was being prepared in the kitchen.

"Unfortunately, we cannot accompany you on your quest, and I am afraid Aegir has already given orders for his soldiers to find you," announced Vor. "We can, however, give you guidance, and we can give you this." Vor removed a golden chain from around her neck, and in one fluid movement, placed it over Claire's head and around her neck.

"I've never seen anything like this," Claire exclaimed. Her hand held tight to the locket. "The details are amazing. Look, Evan, golden flowers are wrapped around the outside. It's beautiful."

"Yes, it is very beautiful. And I suspect you shall

41

never again see one of those," said Vor. "It is a divining locket. It will help you find answers to your questions."

"Thank you," said Claire. "But I can't accept this."

Vor smiled and tilted her head, as if to examine Claire's expression. "How extraordinary it is you would not accept my gift."

"I don't mean to offend you," Claire started, but was cut off by Vor.

"I know. Remember, I know everything," said Vor, gliding through the room. She reclined on an oversized red chair. "You have more need of it than I do; your task is too important. The locket will play an instrumental role in your success on this quest."

"How so?" asked Evan, but Vor didn't answer right away. She just stared off into space.

"Yes, the divining locket will play an important part ... when you least expect it to," said Vor with a smile. "Claire, remove it from your neck only at the appropriate moment. If it were to fall into the wrong hands ... I dare not think it."

"Thank you. How do I use it?" Claire asked.

"First, you must think about what you are about to ask. Be careful when you do this. The locket responds very specifically to questions. Ask your question aloud before opening it. Your answers will come to you through images reflected on the mirror inside. You may ask to see what is happening in the present or you may wish to inquire up to fifty-eight minutes into the future."

"Why fifty-eight minutes?" Evan asked. "I mean, that's a strange number."

"I am Vor, goddess with all knowing power. I cannot allow a simple trinket to hold more power than I have. I should say fifty-eight minutes is very generous."

"It's perfect," said Claire. "Thank you."

"Refreshments are in order. I am certain you will find these to be a tasty treat," said Dr. Irving, motioning toward the six tiers of strange-looking pastries. Arranged neatly on a platter were six glasses, all shaped like inverted pyramids. Each glass held precisely three round ice cubes.

"Professor, what are the red things in center of the ice cubes?" Evan asked.

"Those are razzleberries," Dr. Irving responded and sat next to Vor.

"They are a delicacy. You will not find razzleberries like these outside Asgard," interjected Vor, placing her hand tenderly on Dr. Irving's leg. "I often wonder if they are not the real reason the professor stays."

Dr. Irving laughed with her, all the while participating in some sort of nose kiss. Evan wondered if they had forgotten they had company.

"My goddess is quite the kidder," said the professor, without removing his nose from hers.

"Dear, we mustn't be rude," said Vor.

"Quite right," said Dr. Irving, and without looking away from his wife, he reached for a razzleberry-ice filled glass. From a rectangular pitcher, he poured clear, bubbling liquid into a glass. As the fluid streamed down into the first glass, it changed color. What was once clear was now pink. Dr. Irving handed the drink to Claire, who continued to stare at it.

"Ladies, first," said the professor, as he reached for the second glass. He continued talking about a particular razzleberry patch, remarking how grand those razzleberries were. Evan tried to listen, but couldn't take his eyes off the second glass. The fluid was turning red! The Professor handed it over to Vor.

"Razzleberry flavor for my sweet," he said with a silly grin. Anxiously, Evan watched as Dr. Irving poured the third glass. The clear liquid turned orange. He handed it to Evan and then looked over at Dunkle. "I believe your favorite was mint julep."

"You have quite a memory," said Dunkle, and then he slurped down his green drink.

"Dr. Irving, what are you pouring into our glasses?" Evan asked. "I've never seen liquid change color like that."

"And I doubt you shall, outside of Sagaas," said Dr. Irving, pouring a red-orange fluid into the fifth glass and handing it to Barfel. "This drink is called Fizzy-Whizzle. Its sweetness comes from the nectar of a special flower, found only here in Asgard. A delightful side effect is in its ability to not only change color, but in how it alters its taste to suite each person's preference."

"Amazing," Evan marveled. He then took a swig. "It tastes like orange soda!"

"Mine tastes like cotton candy," exclaimed Claire.

"And I have always enjoyed the taste of grape," said the professor, pouring a dark-purple fluid into his glass.

"Dear, we really must attend to business," Vor reminded. She returned her attention to Evan and Claire. "It won't take long for Aegir to figure out how to use the Serpent's Ring," Vor continued, but had already lost Evan's attention.

Dunkle and Barfel were far more amusing, as they attacked treats with a vengeance. Their movements were so fast, they were a blur. They stuffed their faces with rainbow-colored tarts. Crumbs flew everywhere, landing across the room on a shaggy, white rug. Evan was transfixed by the spectacle and had trouble looking away.

He reached forward and grabbed a round puffed pastry. Unlike the imps, he wasn't going to gobble up the whole thing in one bite; he wanted to enjoy his food. After all, he wasn't sure how long it would be before he could eat again. Besides, he felt manners were in order while in the company of a Norse goddess and an ancient professor.

44

"Excuse me," Evan interrupted. "What is this called?"

"A Poppin-Droppin," Vor said and continued with her tale.

With a strange name like Poppin-Droppin, Evan wasn't sure what to expect. The soft pastry smelled like sweet-cream butter, so he knew it must be good. He shrugged his shoulders and bit it in half. To his delight, the Poppin-Droppin's layers flaked apart, melting in his mouth. Its center was filled with whipped chocolate, delivering the most incredible sensation Evan had ever experienced. That was until the remaining bite in his hand sprouted out another pastry, and then another and another. Poppin-Droppins multiplied, popping out and dropping down so rapidly Evan couldn't catch them. It didn't take long for him to realize how the Poppin-Droppins came by their name.

Dunkle stopped devouring food long enough to say, "You must eat that particular pastry all in one bite; do not leave even a crumb. Otherwise, it will multiply and make a mess."

Evan stuffed Poppin-Droppins in his mouth as quickly as he could. Dunkle and Barfel helped by rapidly shoveling in bouncing pastries. Thank goodness the professor and Vor were too busy talking with Claire to pay much attention to the spectacle.

Evan hoped Claire was listening to Vor's advice closely, because at that moment, he was preoccupied.

CHAPTER SEVEN

POPPIN-DROPPIN AND TALKIN'

" I DON'T UNDERSTAND WHY THE professor didn't keep the Serpent's Ring with him here if it was so important?" Claire asked.

"Long ago, it was decided that all of the great relics needed to be kept hidden and secret," answered Dunkle, "away from the temptation of vengeful gods like Aegir and Ran. Besides, he did not leave the Serpent's Ring unguarded. I have been watching over it since long before you were born." He slunk down, rubbing his hands over his eyes. "Oh, I have lost the ring. What have I done? What have I done?"

This was an extremely awkward moment. Evan realized he should say something, but wasn't sure what. A lump formed in his throat. If only he hadn't been so curious about the professor's secret lab.

Thank goodness, Dr. Irving cut through the tension. "Dunkle, do not blame yourself for what Aegir has done. Why, you watched over the Serpent's Ring successfully for more than a thousand years."

Evan practically dropped his Fizzy-Whizzle. "More than a thousand years? Dunkle, just how old are you?"

"Old. Very, very old," said Dunkle. "And feeling more

46

so every minute that passes without the Serpent's Ring in my care."

"How did you become the protector of the Serpent's Ring in the first place?" Claire asked.

Everyone in the room looked over at Dunkle, who sparkled with recognition. He stepped into the center of the group and began his tale, "Even today, I vividly remember the peaceful years when all the gods were friends and all shared equally the gifts of wisdom and power derived from the Mysticus Orb."

Evan didn't want to interrupt but had to ask, "How long ago are we talking here?"

"Thousands of years have passed since the gods decided to divide the world into realms. You call it Pangaea, but we immortals refer to it as the Avarice Wars. I will never forget the very first time I peered down through the sky and saw the new markings of Terra. You see, in the chaos of the Avarice Wars, the gods tore the world apart, forming new land masses called continents, divided by great bodies of water called oceans."

"But I thought land masses split apart because of shifting in the Earth's tectonic plates," said Claire.

"That is what the gods want for you to believe," Dr. Irving chimed.

"Dunkle, why did the gods go to war against each other?" Evan asked.

Dunkle sighed. "As I said, there was a time when the gods were united and shared a common purpose. There was only one realm, one religion, and one Mysticus Orb. That was until Alamaz, the immortal human, became more and more jealous of the gods' powers. Through a devious plan, Alamaz used clever lies and flattery to set the gods against each other. Then, when the heavens were in chaos, he tried to steal the Mysticus for himself.

"Thankfully, a little band of creatures was able to stop Alamaz just in time. Now, he is locked away in the

Dungeon of Dreadful Dreams, forever more to be guarded by his own worst nightmares.

"The gods realized nothing like this could ever happen again, but they argued about what to do with the Mysticus Orb—where to hide it, who should watch over it. Finally, the golden and mysterious Orb did something unexpected. It rose up, spun around and around, faster and faster. It floated higher and higher, until suddenly it froze. With a blinding flash of light, it crashed thunderously down, splitting into multiple golden spheres. Each sphere rolled toward a different god or goddess and then floated upward. The small globes formed into their own unique design: a golden staff, a band in the shape of a serpent biting its own tail, a totem, and so on.

"Each relic still held the essence of the Mysticus Orb, but each contained its own unique set of powers. The Mysticus had demonstrated its greatness and wisdom, as only it could.

"I recall that all of the gods in attendance stood for a very long time in complete silence. Until at last, a soft voice came from under a beard resembling twilight, both lavender and midnight blue, 'The relics must be kept as far from us as possible, until we are sure we have learned from our mistakes, repaired the damage we have done, and accepted the responsibility for our actions.'

"For the first time in many moons, the gods agreed. And so they assigned honorary guardians, each as unique and diverse as the relics themselves, custody over each of the relics, and they were hidden around the globe.

"There was much healing to be done both in the heavens and on Terra. As a constant reminder, above the entrance to the Celestial Atrium, the gods inscribed:

Let there come a day, when there is peace among all

nations, when every god and every man is grateful for his own gifts, and rejoices equally in the gifts of others. Then, and only then, may the pieces of the Mysticus Orb once more be joined together for the benefit of all.

"I shall never forget those words," Dunkle said and sighed. "Now, after thousands of years, I have failed in my duty."

"Nonsense! You have done a marvelous job watching over the Serpent's Ring, and now you shall retrieve it from Aegir," said Dr. Irving. "Besides, the Mysticus Orb would have been stolen by Alamaz had you not led your little band of heroes to save it."

Dunkle wrapped his hands around his shoulders and hugged himself, as he shed a tear.

"So, you saved the Mysticus Orb from Alamaz?" Evan asked excitedly. "I'd like to hear about how you did that."

"I will share that particular story with you another day," said Dunkle. "I am afraid we are running short on time."

"Wait a minute. Dr. Irving, how did you end up with the Serpent's Ring?" Claire asked.

"That is a very long but interesting story," began Dr. Irving. "After graduating from the university, with a doctorate in botany, I was eager to study the flora of Norway. As soon as I was able, I traveled there. I spent weeks hiking in the fields, mountains, meadows, and fjords of western Norway. Then, one fateful day, as I was sketching a newly discovered specimen into my journal, I heard a terrible blood-curdling scream. It was followed by a waft of the most unusual and rather unpleasant odor. I was glued to the spot, when out from a nearby patch of trees emerged the most pitiful little creature I had ever seen. It was obvious it had been seriously injured; he could barely limp to my feet, and when he did, he collapsed completely.

"At the time, I was unaware he came from another realm. Naturally, I assumed he was a specimen of some unknown origin. I believed I had stumbled upon the discovery of the century, and Dunkle allowed me to remain naive in my assumptions.

"I nursed Dunkle back to health as best I could. But it became obvious, that although the external wounds seemed to be healing, my patient was getting weaker by the day. Then Dunkle gave me the surprise of my life. Here I thought I was taking care of a poor defenseless creature, when all of a sudden, he began to speak!

"'We must return to Asgard,' my strange, little creature whispered. As you can imagine, I literally fell to the floor."

"Here, I had always assumed you startled because of what I said, not because I said anything at all," said Dunkle with a smile.

Dr. Irving continued with his story, "Then, the little creature raised his head, for what I believed must be the last time, and gasped, 'Not much time; please, we will need the Serpent's Ring.'

"I just stared in astonishment, and Dunkle stared right back at me. He shook his head and said, 'Please, excuse my manners; my name is Dunkle. Now, hurry!'

"What was I to do? I gathered Dunkle into my arms and followed his directions to where he had hidden the Serpent's Ring. This was particularly difficult since, as we approached the exact spot, Dunkle made me shield my eyes. I retrieved the Serpent's Ring and was impressed by its intricacy. Although Dunkle was not particularly heavy, our journey had been long, and I needed both hands free to carry him back. Without a thought, I placed the golden ring on my arm. Then something astounding occurred. The sky changed from blue to tangerine."

"You were in Sagaas!" chimed Evan.

"Yes, we were," said Dr. Irving.

"Then what happened?" urged Claire.

"I happened," replied Vor.

With a silly grin, Dr. Irving continued, "Vor nursed Dunkle back to health; the improvement was noticeable immediately. I was amazed by Vor's knowledge of medicinal herbs; there were species here I had never dreamed of, but the real truth was I was captivated by her mind and beauty and fell head over heels in love."

"And you never left Asgard?" asked Claire.

"No, I never did," Dr. Irving said and winked at Vor. "Besides, after touching the Serpent's Ring, I was changed."

"You don't mean to say you also have powers?" Claire asked.

"Yes, that is correct," admitted Dr. Irving. "I am able to transfigure an object and then move it through the air, both with a simple thought."

"Both powers! Wow, that is so cool!" said Evan.

"It can be. But you must use caution when using your powers," Vor added. "And, Evan, you must listen to what your dreams are telling you."

"My goddess is very wise," said Dr. Irving. "You can see why I fell in love with her. If I am to be honest, I forgot all about the Serpent's Ring, but Vor and Dunkle did not. They knew it must be returned to Terra quickly, and as soon as Dunkle was strong enough to travel, he left to find a new location for which to hide it."

"Wait!" said Claire. "Dunkle, how did you get injured in the first place?"

Dunkle shuddered and hugged his body tight with his arms. A strong odor began to fill the space around him.

Vor looked at Dunkle and almost imperceptibly shook her head back and forth; Dr. Irving immediately changed the subject. "Dunkle, I have yet to ask, where did you hide it?"

"Your secret laboratory served as the most proper hiding place," said Dunkle, with great relief. "That was until your entire house was shipped over to America and placed on exhibit."

"Placed on exhibit?" said Dr. Irving. "But why on Terra would anyone be interested in seeing my old home?"

Evan interjected, "Are you kidding me? That lab of yours is awesome! I could spend days digging through all of your things."

"I am also afraid that your sudden disappearance caused quite some commotion," said Dunkle. "You are famous."

"I am famous because I disappeared, not for my research and ideas," stated the Professor. "Unfortunate, really—I would much rather be famous for something more notable."

"I should never have entered your house, much less removed the Serpent's Ring," said Evan.

"Do not place blame," Vor interrupted. "What was done was done. Now, we need to focus our efforts on finding the Serpent's Ring and returning it back to your world."

"How will we be able to do this?" Claire asked.

"You must sail south to the island, Hlesey. It sits above the Undersea Hall of Aegir and Ran. I am afraid, you have only three days in which to retrieve the Serpent's Ring," said Vor.

"But why only three days?" Evan asked.

"Because, that is when the mighty sea serpent's head will travel over Asgard, of course," said Vor.

"Dear, our guests are probably not aware of Jormundgand's cycle," Dr. Irving whispered into her ear.

"Really, I simply assumed everyone knew of Jormundgand's cycle," said Vor, returning her attention toward Evan and Claire. "You see, not only is Jormundgand wrapped around Terra, he circles it just like the rings around Saturn."

"Jormundgand is so big he actually circles the entire planet?" Evan asked.

"Of course," said Vor.

"Exactly how big is his body, and how big is his head?" Evan questioned.

"His body is rather thin, about the size around as one of your cruise ships," explained Vor. "His head is much larger, but you shall see that soon enough."

"How much larger are we talking about here?" Evan asked.

"Evan, the size of Jormundgand is not relevant," said Vor. "It is important for you to focus on how you will retrieve the Serpent's Ring from Aegir."

"How are we supposed to do that?" Evan asked.

"You must enter through his Undersea Hall without his knowledge; however, that will be tricky," said Vor.

"How will we be able to?" Claire asked.

Vor smiled. "You will discover new friends along the way. You will find help in places you least expect."

"At last, some good news. Vague, but good," said Evan.

Vor stared at the siblings, as if contemplating. "Your powers are stronger in Sagaas. Be careful when you use them. They will help save you from trouble, but they could steer you off course."

"What is that supposed to mean?" Evan asked, but Vor continued to hold a blank expression.

"She does this when she 'sees.' You will have to decode the information yourself. That is how it usually works," whispered Dr. Irving.

And just when Evan was really intrigued, it was time to leave.

CHAPTER EIGHT

TROLLS AND SNOW GLOBES

"**Y**OU MUST MAKE HASTE," SAID Dr. Irving. "I am afraid Aegir has been alerted to your arrival. You see, when you touched the Serpent's Ring, an energy wave was sent throughout all of Sagaas."

"Pay close attention when you enter the forest," said Vor. "You do not want to face what lurks among the trees at night. Remember, if you need answers, look into the divining locket. It will serve as your guide."

"Farewell, my old friend," Dr. Irving said and squeezed Dunkle, lifting him from the floor. "Good luck and much success on your quest."

"You will be safe once you reach the ship," said Vor, "at least for tonight. Be ever diligent while at sea. There will be spies, those who wish for Aegir to flood these lands. Be careful; Aegir has mercenaries searching for you."

"What kind of mercenaries?" Evan asked.

"He has enlisted various creatures of the most unsavory nature: trolls and giants. He has promised them great rewards. I am afraid your voyage will be difficult."

"Thank you for your help," said Claire diplomatically.

She then turned toward her brother. "We need to hurry."

As the small group treaded along winding corridors, Evan ran his fingertips along and over the knobby wooden walls. Up ahead, a pale-blue light trickled through a small gap. Dunkle rushed over and knocked in a rhythmic beat. The crevice widened, and the group exited the tree.

The sky had turned to twilight, with hazy clouds reflecting purple, blue, and orange. Tiny fragments of light whizzed by like fireflies feasting on flowers. A golden beam zipped through the grass and froze a few inches from Evan's face. Its little body was four inches tall with wings that sparkled and glowed. She—it must have been a she—wore a small band of leaves around her spiky red hair. Evan wasn't sure what she was, but one thing he knew for certain, she definitely wasn't a firefly.

"Hi there," said Evan. She fluttered around him in multiple circles with a stream of light trailing behind her and then she disappeared. "Ouch! She set fire to the back of my neck! Where did she go?" He shouted, flailing his arms around his head.

"I'm sure she didn't do it on purpose," Claire said and leaned toward the pixie, whispering sweetly, "Don't listen to him. I won't let him hurt you." Just then, another fairy swooped down from a tree branch and pelted Claire's forehead with an acorn. "Hey! That hurt!" yelled Claire, trying to grab the tiny menace.

"I'm sure it was an accident," Evan said smugly and laughed.

"What did you expect her to do, grant you a wish?" said Dunkle. "Why should she treat you kindly? She does not owe you anything. Besides, you will find most creatures in Sagaas are upset with humans."

Dunkle looked at the red-headed fairy and made a funny sound and wriggled with his ears. The fairy dashed to the side of his head, hovered for a second, and just like that, she was gone.

"What did she say?" Evan asked, still rubbing the back of his neck.

"Oh, nothing much, just giving me some news," said Dunkle, turning toward the trail. "We need to watch out for trolls."

"Trolls," repeated Claire. "Come on, let's go." She grabbed Evan's arm and raced for the ship.

Although their ship was somewhat camouflaged, stars reflected along its surface, helping the group find it easily enough. The imps had started to climb aboard when a loud thump came from aboard the vessel. Dunkle and Barfel zipped away so swiftly that Evan barely saw them run off.

"They're close. I can smell 'em," said a wet, soggy voice, coming from aboard the vessel. "Go down and find 'em, we will."

Evan whispered to Claire, "Those trolls are onboard. Ugh, gross! That one has three ugly heads. Look, the other troll is wearing my hat. What are we going to do?"

"I'm not sure, but we need to get on the boat," said Claire. Adding sarcastically, "But first, we need to find our great imp protectors."

"Good idea." Evan edged backward and then quickened his stride. But just as he turned around, *wham!* He slammed right into a big troll with a humongous nose!

"Ugh," Evan yelped and backed away. The troll reached out his hairy arm and grabbed hold of Evan's T-shirt. "Claire, run for it!"

But Claire hadn't run two steps before another large troll snatched her up and off the ground. "Aahh!" Claire squealed, kicking and pounding. She was face to faces with a three-headed troll! Stringy, greasy hair dangled from each of its heads. Each face was a different shade of yellow. One was greenish-yellow, the other an orange-yellow, and the third a yellowish-gray. Worst of all, their skin was covered with cherry-size boils!

"What we gots here?" Evan's troll grumbled.

"It looks like we gots what we was after," said the center head of Claire's troll, still using his free hand to block her punches. "Hey, Grot, I gots meself a feisty one. Think Aegir will let us eat 'em? It look tasty."

Evan's troll answered, "Mighty tasty, but we was told no hurt 'em. Aegir wants 'em unspoiled, so he can deal with 'em 'imself."

"Just one lil' bite won't hurt 'em," said the head on the far left, saliva dripping from between his green teeth.

"Not one bite! We deliver 'em unharmed, an' we'll get lots of other tasty bites," said Grot.

"An' when the flood come, there be tons of chewy bits floatin'," said the troll's right head. As he stared at Claire's shoulder, drool poured down like syrup onto her arm.

"Put me down!" Claire managed to yell, wiping her arm on the troll's ratty shirtsleeve.

Whoa, things were intense; Evan had to come up with a plan and fast! He looked around and realized the only thing within reach was a bunch of golden sand, golden shells, and golden pebbles.

"Those will have to do," Evan mumbled and then concentrated.

Golden sand swirled around. Small rocks and shells joined into the mix, forming a small tornado. The whirlwind stretched higher and faster. Claire's troll turned, let out a cry, and then flung up his arms, shielding his three faces. At last, Claire fell to the ground. She focused on the area around the troll's dirt-encrusted toenails, and before Evan knew it, the sand was so thick that all three of the troll's heads disappeared from sight.

The sand transformed into great bubbles of gooey glass and then formed an enormous sphere. It didn't take long for the troll to become imprisoned.

Now Evan had to free himself from his troll. There were tiny pebbles scattered along the shore. Evan used them to pelt his troll on the back of his head. Evan's pirate hat flew off the troll and landed on the ground. When the troll lifted his hands to protect his eyes, Evan fell to freedom and scurried over to retrieve his hat. Claire trapped the second troll within another shimmering glass prison. Bits of golden sand fluttered around inside, which made Evan think he was looking into an enormous snow globe.

Both trolls screeched and bellowed and pleaded to be released. The troll's right head yelled, "Ouch! Stings!"

The troll's left head cried out, "We be turn to stone when sun ups the morning!"

"No leave us!" hollered the troll's center face.

"You'll get what you deserve. How could you try to eat us?" said Evan, now standing on the ship's deck and leaning over its side.

"Nooo," they continued to cry, and Evan felt somewhat sorry for the wretched creatures.

"Come on; let's set sail," said Claire, not even glancing over at the trolls. She lifted her nose and sniffed. While cringing, she pivoted on her heels and stared down. Glaring at the two imps, she added, "Gee, glad you could make it back."

"Eeww, you must have been really scared. You guys stink!" declared Evan, grabbing his nose and fanning the air.

"We feel awful for leaving you," mumbled Dunkle.

"What else could we do, could we do?" said Barfel.

"Oh, I don't know. How about, stay and help us fight?" said Evan.

"Just look what you two accomplished. Why, you

outwitted trolls," said Dunkle.

"Three cheers for Evan and Claire!" Barfel chimed, and his wretched odor returned to the more pleasant cedar scent.

"We need to be able to count on you," interjected Claire. "You can't run off every time things get a little scary. Not if we're going to beat Aegir."

Dunkle and Barfel glanced at each other and nodded.

"You are right. Generally speaking, imps are not afraid of many things; unfortunately, we are not particularly fond of trolls. We find their odor rather repulsive and, how can I put this delicately, it causes imps to lose their breakfast. However, we will not abandon you again," Dunkle said with a grin, and he too began to smell a whole lot better.

"All right, I'm counting on that," Claire said and headed to the back of the boat.

Evan used his powers to return the ship to water. Their vessel floated over waves and sliced through the current. The mainland disappeared from view, and Evan watched Claire wave her hand around like she was swatting a fly.

"I couldn't leave the trolls like that, even if they are stupid and stinky," she said, and Evan could hear the sound of glass shattering.

CHAPTER NINE

COW SAYS: "MOO"

THAT NIGHT, AS EVAN CURLED into a ball on the boat's deck, he had another bad dream. In it, he was sailing the glass Viking ship, alone; everything was calm. That was until a huge thump pounded from underneath. Evan looked down past his sneakers and through the clear deck. Something shifted in the dark-blue water below. A gigantic stingray appeared, gliding along. Peacefully, it streamed through the water. It began to swim faster and faster, and then more arrived. They pushed and knocked and banged into the boat.

"Come to me, come to me. I will keep you safe," a delicate song reached Evan's ears. "Come to me, come to me."

Evan was transfixed by the melody. Frantically, he scanned the horizon. But no one was there. Wait! There, on top of a coral reef sat a beautiful woman. A ring of flowers was perched upon her long golden hair; she wore it as if it were an imperial crown. She didn't move her lips, but from her came an enchanting melody. Her shoulders swayed, and her fingers rolled back toward her palm. Desperately, Evan maneuvered around the stingrays—he wanted to be near the enchantress.

Closer, closer … she was almost within reach. A few more yards, and he would be able to join her. Almost there! Her smile was sweet and enchanting. Evan's heart melted. Her milky-white arms extended toward him. As he was gazing into her pale-blue eyes, he noticed a cow's tale appear from behind her back. Without warning, her song changed into a high screech! It pierced Evan's ears and vibrated through his bones. He clasped his hands to the sides of his head and screamed.

※

"Aahh!" Evan cried out and sat upright.

"Evan, Evan, wake up. You're having another nightmare," Claire's voice called to him, as she shook his shoulders.

Evan opened his eyes. Dunkle and Barfel were hunching forward, wringing their hands, and Claire sat back with a sigh. "You really scared me. What were you dreaming about?"

"I just had a bad dream. I'll be alright," he said and pulled himself up off the deck. He peered over the bow: no sharks, no stingrays, and no sea cows.

He then looked out toward the horizon; the sun had arrived as a pale-yellow ball. It rose up into the dark-blue sky, and its yellow center intensified, deepening in color.

Evan leaned his body back against the boat's side and clenched his stomach. "I'm hungry. I don't suppose we have any reserve food left?"

"I'm afraid not. Wait, I have an idea," said Claire, leaning down to lift a piece of driftwood. The stick stretched into a long pole.

Evan reached for it, exclaiming, "It's a fishing pole! We need a line and lure."

"No problem," said Claire. She stared up at the sail and some thread unraveled. Evan guided the thread across the ship and then attached it to the rod. She scooped up a tiny ball of glass and molded it into a lure—shiny and desirable to any fish.

"That will do," said Evan, casting the line.

Within a matter of seconds, he felt a tug. Skillfully, he set the hook. "I caught one!" he yelled, pulling in his prize. "And it's big!"

Claire created a net from another piece of driftwood and more blue thread. This fish was fat, 30 pounds or more. It took both Claire and Evan to bring it in.

"I don't believe it," said Evan, watching the fish flip and flop.

"I know. You caught a fish," said Claire, "a pretty one too."

"No, I mean the colors are familiar. Just like the sharks and stingrays in my dream," he said, still studying the patterns on the fish's scaly skin. "Dunkle, is it normal for fish to have this kind of marking?"

"Only those loyal to Aegir have colors like that," said Dunkle. "I am afraid you caught one of his spies."

Evan's face paled, and he said, "I've lost my appetite. What do we do with *it*?"

"We'll take care of *him*," said Dunkle, retrieving the fish. "Claire, we will need your help, if you please."

She followed the imps to the back of the boat. Evan watched as they explained something to her. Barfel handed her a glass shield and backed away. The shield transformed into a rectangular glass tub. Dunkle lowered a bucket into the ocean and filled it with seawater; he then poured the water into the tub. Swiftly, Barfel dumped in the colorful fish.

Claire returned and sat beside Evan. The two imps made horrible squawking sounds, barely pausing to take a breath. After a few minutes, they looked at each other and nodded.

Dunkle hollered toward Evan and Claire, "Aegir

knows we are here for the Serpent's Ring. He will do everything in his power to stop us."

"Are you going to let the fish go?" Claire asked.

"We might need him," said Dunkle, tapping his hand along the side of the glass fish tank. "If he helps us enough, we might let him go."

Evan stretched his neck and looked down through the glass bottom. Colorful fish multiplied below.

"Claire, do you hear that?" Evan asked, his eyes developing a milky-white film.

"I don't hear anything," said Claire, also looking around.

"That song, it's so beautiful. I heard it in my dream," said Evan as if hypnotized. "Mooo-ooooo, moooo-ooooo."

"Evan, you sound like a cow. And all I hear is wind in the sail," she said and peered over the bow. The imps scurried over and joined her in the search.

"Oh dear, oh dear!" squealed Barfel, and the pleasant odor of cedar disappeared, replaced by something awful.

"What's going on?" Claire asked in alarm.

"It must be Huldra. Her call can be heard only by men. That is why you and we cannot hear it," Dunkle explained.

"Who's Huldra?" Claire asked.

"I have never met her, but I have heard she is an extremely beautiful woman," said Dunkle.

"Well, that doesn't sound so bad," said Claire.

"I would not be so sure about that, not unless the man does not mind loving a woman who has the tail of a cow. And with her, most men do not mind. She will lure the man into worshiping her and then she changes," said Dunkle.

"How so?"

"She turns into a frightening old hag, with the strength of ten men. If she traps Evan, I am afraid he is done for," said Dunkle.

"What do we do? I don't see anything!" screamed Claire. "What is she doing here in the middle of the ocean?"

"Aegir has requested help from many creatures," Dunkle quipped. "Do not be surprised by anything."

"It's the most incredible music I've ever heard. Moo-ooo-oooo," sang Evan. "I must head over in that direction."

"Bad idea, bad idea! Not that way!" shouted out Barfel, leaping toward the back of the boat. He grabbed the rudder and strained to break Evan's control over the ship. Evan was strong, but in his current hypnotic trance, Barfel was stronger and able to shift direction just in time. Rocks, shaped like giant swords, jutted out of the sea!

More and more gray spikes appeared far below the clear ship, ready to pierce through the hull. Bubbles multiplied, obscuring the view of the deep sea and spikes. Again, Barfel shifted direction. Now, they were heading back toward Dr. Irving's home.

"We can't go back! That's what Aegir wants us to do!" yelled Claire. She reached Evan and shook him vigorously. "Evan, Evan, snap out of it! We need your help!"

His eyes were hidden behind a cloudy film. Claire looked around desperately. She spied Barfel's shell collection and rushed over. She rummaged through the little pile and removed two clamshells.

"They're a little small but will have to do," she said and returned to Evan.

The shells grew bigger, ballooning out, and then deflating so as to fit snugly over Evan's ears. She continued to shake him, while screaming in his face. At last, his blue-green eyes returned.

"What happened?" he asked.

"Rocks are blocking our path! It's going to take both

of us to get through!" she said and lifted him to his feet.

"What do we do?" he asked, thumping his hand on the side of his head. "What's on my ears?"

He tried to pull off the shells, but Claire grabbed his hands and shook her head no. "Leave them on! Trust me!"

"But I can barely hear you!" cried out Evan.

"Believe me; you don't want to be able to hear."

Evan stared ahead. One hand gripped the boat's side, while the other clasped his sister. He was ready to charge.

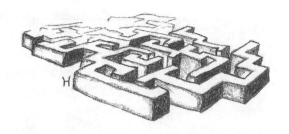

CHAPTER TEN

BINDING BRONZE

"BARFEL, TURN US AROUND!" CLAIRE commanded, and Barfel did as instructed. "Evan, on my signal, speed us up. Make the ship fly if you can. We must get around those rocks."

Claire strained her eyes, searching for a clear pathway. The ocean gurgled like boiling oil and bubbles burst on its surface. Rocks followed and sharp edges now blocked their way. Claire squinted and the rocks began to bend, forming a circular tunnel.

"Evan, now!" yelled Claire.

The boat lunged forward, moving through the warped formations, but just as Evan managed to push the boat forward, the current would drag it back. Had the sea actually grown tentacles?

"Evan, try to lift the boat higher!" shouted Claire.

Evan closed his eyes and focused on lifting the ship. The sea's tentacles stretched higher and higher, until finally, Evan heard a strange *POP*. The boat jarred back, but Evan managed to push it forward and raced over the water.

Ultimately, the ship moved faster than the rocks could form, and before long, the rocks were nowhere in sight. And although air beat at his face, he refused to slow down. He propelled the boat as far forward as he could before finally resting and allowing the boat to drift along the calm water.

"We made it!" Claire cheered, wrapping her arms around her brother. She hugged him tightly, but pulled away quickly. "Uh, good job, Evan. And here, let me remove those clam shells from your ears."

"Yes, well done, Evan. Unfortunately it seems we have one little problem," said Dunkle. "We have gotten ourselves off-track."

"Well, that's all right. We'll just go back a little," said Evan.

"I'm afraid it's going to be more than just a little. We overshot Hlesey completely. It will take an entire day to return," said Dunkle.

"No biggie. I'll just zip us back," said Evan. "But I'm tired and need to rest for a minute first."

Dunkle stepped forward, saying, "Not a good idea. You will need to rest for more than a minute to be able to use your powers again."

"I feel okay, just a little sleepy," said Evan.

"Evan, your powers have limits," explained Dunkle. "It is best if you do not exhaust yourself. You will need your strength for when you meet Aegir."

Barfel leapt into the middle of the group. "Another island! Just that way! Just that way!"

"Good thing," said Claire. "We need to get off this boat. Maybe, we'll be able to find some *edible* food."

"All food is *edible*, Claire," Evan mocked.

Claire glanced over to where the colorful fish-spy was still imprisoned. His large bulging eyes stared at them through his fish-tank prison.

"Not really," she said and cringed.

Barfel was right. Halfway through the day, an island appeared in the distance.

"We shouldn't spend much time on that island," Dunkle said and shivered, a faint musty odor wafted.

"Dunkle, what is *that* island?" Evan asked, pinching his nose.

"It is called Jotunheim, land of giants," Dunkle answered.

"Great—so there are actual giants on that island?" Claire asked.

Dunkle and Barfel both nodded. As they drew closer to the island, the foul odor of decay drifted in their direction. Evan and Claire both turned their heads toward the imps.

"Not us! Not us! Giants!" cried out Barfel.

"Not good," Evan said to Claire. "Wanna use some of Barfel's shells to make a cover for my nose?"

"Man up, Evan. Stop being such a sissy," she said.

Evan raised the boat onto shore, and the crew leapt overboard. Evan had no desire to scoop up this sand, with its dark-greenish color and rank odor of mildew. He dragged his feet through sludge with bits of animal remains. Skull fragments were here and rib bones were there. And the dunes were covered with graying sea oats.

"Barfel, hurry up!" Claire yelled toward the straggling imp.

"What's he doing back there?" Evan asked.

"It looks like he's saying something to that fish-spy. That imp better hurry up," said Claire. "I don't want to wait around here for too long. The sooner we find food, the sooner we can leave this horrible place."

"This island is pretty disgusting," Evan agreed.

Beyond the dunes, a patch of lush emerald-green grass sprouted up from the dead ground. Trees burst into life and fruit swelled like balloons on long branches.

"Perfect!" shouted Evan, quickening his pace.

"Wait! Things aren't always what they seem," yelled Dunkle. But Evan was too fast. He and Claire were halfway up to the plump luscious fruit when wilted and battered vines came to life. They grew fast, intertwining and creating knots that formed into walls of a labyrinth. A tightly woven barricade formed and separated the imps from Evan and Claire.

"It's a trap! It's a trap!" Barfel shouted from somewhere beyond the tall hedges.

"Don't move; we'll find you!" yelled Claire.

"Argh!" Dunkle's wail was followed by pounding and shuffling.

"Dunkle? Barfel?" said Claire in a shaky whisper.

Nothing, no response.

"What do you suppose happened?" Evan asked.

"I don't know. But we need to find them."

"Of course, but I'm starving. I'm going to pass out if I don't eat soon, and that pear looks delicious."

Evan wrapped his hand around a succulent looking pear. It felt soft and ripe. With a gentle tug, he released it from the tree, and Evan claimed his prize. Just as he brought the golden fruit to his mouth it started to harden. It had turned to brass or maybe copper. He tossed the hunk of metal aside and reached for a pear with yellow and orange skin. But it too transformed into metal.

"I don't believe it! What kind of sick joke is this?" shouted Evan. "When am I going to eat?"

"You need to be patient. We'll find food after we find the imps," said Claire, reaching for the wall of ivy. When she tugged and pushed at the vines, they too transformed into metal. "Whoa, what's happening?" she asked and tried to tear through the wall. "Ouch!" She pulled away and stuck her finger in her mouth.

"Are you bleeding?" Evan asked, not daring to look. Instead, he focused on a patch of ivy still green with life.

"So, you touched the wall, and the vines changed into metal?"

"Yeah. It's unbelievably sharp; it sliced me pretty good," mumbled Claire, her finger still inserted in her mouth.

"So I guess that means we won't be able to climb over these walls," said Evan, looking up at all of the surrounding plant life.

The pounding returned, and the ground shook. Could it possibly be an elephant? Unfortunately, it was not an elephant, but a group of enormous hairy men! Their bodies were covered with clothes made from animal skins. Massive battle armor—clubs with spikes, axes, swords, and knives—rattled at their sides.

"Run!" Claire screamed, grabbing hold of Evan's arm. They fled down one of the labyrinth's long pathways, but after only a few feet were stopped short. Two giants were blocking their way!

Claire did not touch the wall; instead, she focused her mental powers on the ivy. The vines melted together like wax from a candle. Eventually, an opening stretched wide enough for Evan and Claire to squeeze through safely. In a flash, Claire resealed the hole behind them.

More and more giants came at them from just a few yards away. Claire continued to create passageways through the ivy, but it was no use. They were outnumbered. Evan's heart sank, and he stared down at the dirt beneath his sneakers. He kicked at a tiny pebble. It scuttled over the ground and then floated up into the air. Just then, a radical idea came to him. An idea he wasn't so certain would work.

"Claire, hold on to me tight," he said and looked up toward the open sky. "I'm not exactly sure how this will go."

"How what will go? Evan, what are you going to doooo—" Claire began, but her feet were pulled off the ground! Within seconds, she and Evan were soaring above the clan of giants who were swinging their clubs around. Claire kicked her legs, whacking one giant on his nose. As the siblings rose up higher and higher, the giants continued to yell, holler, and raise their fists.

Evan followed the lines of the maze. There, in its center, sat a dilapidated fort with high crumbling walls. Off to the right was a crumbling tower, propped up with large wooden beams.

"Look, there's Dunkle," said Claire, pointing toward a broken drawbridge that hung over a parched moat.

Three large giants clutched the tiny imps, who were kicking and thrashing their little bodies. But the imps were no match for giants and were eventually taken inside the fort's stone walls.

A giant's booming voice echoed. "Why bring imps? Where humans?"

Evan swooped down and hovered outside.

"They were, uh, got away," answered another giant.

"Find humans!" thundered a commanding voice. "Aegir be angry if we don't hand over humans. And giants drown wit rest of 'em."

"Yeah, me no wanna drown, cuz measly kids got away," said a third giant. "Hounds find 'em. I go open crate."

"They're releasing hounds. Evan, get us out of here," Claire demanded, and Evan lifted them up and away.

A sinister mountain loomed up ahead. Its entire surface consisted of chiseled rock—sharp and uninviting. A severe point at its top and a moss-covered cave gaped open in the middle.

"We can hide out over there. Just until we figure out a plan," said Claire.

Evan looked over at the cave. Smoke streamed out from its mouth, as if it were alive and hungry. He shuddered and asked, "Are you sure about this?"

"Do you have a better idea?"

"Good point."

They flew ahead and hovered over a plateau of barren wasteland. An unrecognizable odor came from inside the cave. They touched ground, and a tremendous sound erupted.

"What was that?" Evan questioned.

"I don't know," said Claire. "I think it came from behind those boulders."

Suddenly, a man emerged, staggering toward them. "Run! The beast is coming!" he shouted and stumbled to the ground.

"Claire, give me your hand. We need to fly out of here," yelled Evan, but Claire was already too far away. She rushed to help the dark-haired man.

"You have no time to help me! Quick, you must go inside the cave!" cried out the man.

Claire paid no attention to the man's words and stubbornly helped him to his feet. He limped and was obviously in pain. She allowed him to use her shoulder as a crutch and the two hobbled toward the cave.

"Here you go," said Claire, resting the man gently on the ground.

"Thank you. You have saved me from that wretched creature," said the man, gripping his hand around his knee.

Evan continued to listen for the beast, but couldn't hear anything. Nothing. Not even a gust of wind.

"Whatever was following you seemed to have gone," said Evan, approaching Claire and the injured man.

"I would not be so foolish to believe Bergkonge has vanished. He will hunt until he finds what he is after," said the man.

"What is a Bergog or whatever?" Evan asked.

"Bergkonge is the Mountain King. He enjoys enticing young women away from their path. He brings them to his mountain and they are never heard from again," said the man.

"How is he able to seduce women? I mean, I wouldn't exactly follow a horrible monster up a mountain," said Claire.

The man grinned and said, "He does not look like a beast when he meets these women. It is said that he is extremely handsome. Besides, women are easily fooled."

"Not this woman. You have to be pretty slick to pull one over on me," said Claire.

Just then, a scuffling sound came from outside the cave. Claire jumped to her feet, and said, "Evan, I think the dragon is out there."

"But, Claire, it doesn't sound like a dragon."

"Oh, and you know what a dragon sounds like?" scoffed Claire.

CHAPTER ELEVEN

BEST-KEPT SECRET

"**S**TOP! YOU ARE NO MATCH for Bergkonge," said the man. "You need to stay inside the cave where you are safe. The dragon is far too large to enter this cave. His wing span alone is as wide as a ship."

"Well, if Bergkonge can change into a man, then obviously, he can enter this cave. We need to come up with a plan," said Claire, trying to peer outside. "I don't see anything out there."

"That is probably because there is nothing out there to worry about," said the man. But instead of sounding weak and feeble, his voice was now smooth and cunning. "You were lured so easily into this cave."

Evan and Claire turned. Now, the man stood easily. His broad chest was heaving and his shoulders were high and square. His body was draped in a brown cape made from dried leaves. Evan reached for his sister and shuffled back. Strange; the man didn't follow. Why was he standing there with that evil smile, licking his lips?

Suddenly, his mouth stretched forward and his teeth grew longer. His arms shot out, and he lunged forward. With a horrendous snap, his body elongated. His head twisted and distorted and howled!

74

"Come on, Claire. Move!" strained Evan, tugging on his sister's shirt-sleeve.

"Wha-what's happening?" stammered Claire.

"Let's go!" snapped Evan.

Without turning away from the horrific beast, they backed out of the cave. Bergkonge, now fully transformed, followed gleefully. The setting sun outside revealed the full terror of the creature.

The skin on his underside was burnt orange, but as his scales wrapped around to his back, they became red as blood. A coal-black tail trailed back twenty-five feet or more. His wings were held tight to his body, but Evan had no doubt Bergkonge could fly fast and furious. Tufts of wiry hair were behind each ankle, under his chin, and curled around ears that angled back. And the worst part, his bones protruded out, stretching through his skin.

Evan stood in front of Claire, preparing for action. But Bergkonge was too fast. With one swift movement, he knocked Evan aside. Claire stood alone, face to face with a very hungry-looking dragon.

"Look out!" another man's voice sounded from behind.

Claire was pushed aside, just as Bergkonge pounced.

A young man leapt between Claire and the fire-breathing monster. A strange growling sound came from the blond man's throat. The dragon growled back. It actually sounded as if the two were communicating.

Claire was still kneeling on the ground, spitting dirt, and wiping her face. The dragon's attention shifted from Blondielocks back to Claire. Bergkonge growled louder and shuffled closer. Claire lifted her head and her eyes widened. She scooted away, but the dragon followed. And when he snarled, his forked tongue licked across his pointy teeth and smoke rings seethed from his nose.

"Hold very still," instructed Blondielocks. "Most likely, Bergkonge will not attack if you do not move."

"What do you mean most likely? I don't like the sound

of that," said Claire.

"Trust me. I will encourage Bergkonge to go back into the cave," said Blondielocks.

"Why should I trust you?" Claire asked, scooting away from Blondielocks. "I trusted Bergkonge and look where that got me."

"I am nothing like Bergkonge," said Blondielocks.

Evan froze. His sister was in serious trouble, and he had to formulate a plan. He raised his hand and levitated some rocks over the dragon's head. They hovered momentarily and then with one swift motion of his fingers, Evan dropped the rocks. But as they made contact with the dragon's scaly head, they just crumbled into dust. The impact was explosive, but Bergkonge barely flinched.

"What am I supposed to do now?" yelled Evan. "This isn't working!"

"Encourage him to return to the cave," instructed Blondielocks.

"All right, if you insist, I'll 'encourage' Bergkonge," Evan said and focused on the ground. Pebbles started to vibrate and bounce. They sprung up higher and higher, until finally, they began to spiral and twist. Evan created a mini whirlwind, which sucked in more tiny particles of dirt and small stones. It expanded and grew larger and larger. Evan's rock storm towered higher than the dragon. It circled around and around Bergkonge before darting right into his eyes! A thundering roar erupted, and Bergkonge staggered back toward the cave. Grains of dirt continued to pelt his face. He flailed from side to side while whimpering loudly. Evan wasn't sure whether he should fear Bergkonge or feel sorry for him.

When the dragon disappeared from view completely, Claire stretched her fingers outward. As she squeezed them into tight fists, the cave's opening sealed shut, leaving just enough room for the dragon to breathe.

Blondielocks watched from a few yards away, an expression of complete amazement on his face. Claire and Evan stumbled toward each other, checking themselves for any bodily damage as they moved.

"Are you all right?" Evan asked. "I thought you were a goner."

"Me too," said Claire, wiping a smudge off Evan's shirt sleeve. "Thanks."

"It was nothing," Evan said arrogantly and smiled. "Just don't clean my shirt too much. I'd like to keep a few battle marks."

Blondielocks approached, and Evan noticed, for the first time, that he wore unusual clothes: brown loose-fitting pants with a long tunic, high brown boots, and a leather belt strapped around his waist. And worst of all, he had shoulder-length blond hair tied back with a leather strap—too Viking-like for Evan's taste.

"How did you do that?" Blondielocks asked; his sky-blue eyes fixed on Claire.

"Why do you want to know?" asked Claire.

"You still do not trust me," stated Blondielocks. "I suppose after your encounter with Bergkonge that would be understandable. In time, you will learn to trust me."

"Look, no offense, but we're not spending any more time with you or anybody else we happen to meet," said Claire.

"You must be a goddess," said Blondielocks. He approached Claire, staring at her with complete admiration.

Claire giggled and looked down. "No, I'm not a goddess," she responded while pushing a few strands of hair behind her ear.

"Then who are you?" he asked.

"I'm sorry, but I'm not going to tell you," said Claire. "Evan, we really need to leave."

Evan rolled his eyes and interrupted, "My name is

Evan, and this is my sister, Claire. We're from Michigan."

"Michigan? It must be an enchanting realm," said the man, still gazing at Claire. "I am Sigurd, an immortal human, but human nonetheless."

"You're not related to Alamaz, are you?" asked Claire.

Sigurd blanched with horror. "I should think not!"

"What are you doing on this island? I sure do hope you don't live here," said Evan.

"I have been tracking Bergkonge," Sigurd responded.

"What do you plan to do with him?" Claire asked, raising her head.

"I plan to relocate him."

"So, you aren't going to kill him?" Claire asked.

"No. I will take him to an island far away, where he will not be able to hurt anyone again," said Sigurd.

"Where's your SWAT team? Surely, you're not planning to capture and move that dragon all by yourself," said Evan.

"I have captured many dragons," said Sigurd.

"How?" said Claire. "I mean, that must be very dangerous."

"Dragons tend to be extremely destructive and cannot be near villages. Up until a few years ago, they were everywhere. People were losing their homes, many lost their lives. I discovered quickly enough that I am quite good at tracking and trapping dragons." Sigurd laughed. "The last one I hunted burned down half a town before I was able to subdue her. But that is another story."

"That sounds fascinating!" said Claire.

Evan interjected, "Another time. Remember, Claire, we need to find Dunkle and Barfel." Evan then reached for his sister and looked over at Sigurd. "Thanks for your help. Bye!"

"Perhaps, I can help you. Who is this Dunkle?" Sigurd asked.

"He and Barfel are imps," informed Claire. "We were

separated by a wall of vines and then these giant men took them."

"It would be far too dangerous for you to enter that fort alone. Please, let me come with you," said Sigurd. "I would consider it an honor."

"If you insist, then of course you may join us," blurted Claire, as her face turned pink. "To be honest, we have absolutely no idea what to do next."

"Claire, I thought you weren't going to trust this guy," said Evan.

"Well, I don't," said Claire. "But, let's face it, we need help."

"I am glad you accept my offer. And, my fair lady, I shall prove to you that I am someone you can trust."

"We'll just have to see about that," said Claire, almost flirtatiously.

"I am looking forward to it," said Sigurd, edging closer and closer to Claire.

"What do you suggest we do?" Evan asked.

"Although giants are large, their brains are small. We will be able to outsmart them," said Sigurd. "First, we need to figure out the best way to travel through the labyrinth. It will be dark soon, and even in the daylight, it is extremely tricky," said Sigurd, starring toward the maze of vines.

"That's not a problem," said Claire. "Evan can fly us over it."

"You can fly, boy?" Sigurd turned to face Evan.

"I'm not a boy. And yes, I can fly us down there. Problem solved," stated Evan.

"Both of you are truly astounding. After we find your imps, I would like to know more about your powers and how you came by them."

"Like I said, you'll have to earn our trust first," said Claire.

"I shall do whatever it takes," said Sigurd.

"Is that so?" said Claire, her lashes fluttering a mile a minute.

"Can we focus on saving the imps?" interrupted Evan.

"Of course," Sigurd said with a charming smile. "They are most likely in the tower."

"Wait a minute," said Claire, revealing her golden necklace. Vor's divining locket glowed, as if anxious to help. "We haven't even tried to use this yet."

"Have you figured out how it works?" Evan asked. "I mean, Vor didn't exactly give very detailed instructions."

"Is that a seer?" Sigurd asked.

"Have you ever used one of these?" Claire questioned him.

"No. They are very rare, but I have heard of their powers."

"Great! Maybe you can help me figure out how to make it work," said Claire.

"I can try, but I am not sure I will be of much help. Magical objects are not really my area of expertise."

"Oh, really? What is your area of expertise?" Claire asked, somewhat innocently, and then giggled.

"Claire, focus," interjected Evan.

"Right," she said, then opened the locket. She cupped it in her hands and inhaled. "Here goes nothing. Where are Dunkle and Barfel imprisoned?"

Colors swirled on the glasslike surface—pinks, yellows, purples. The image was blurry, at first, but finally the imps came into view. They were bound and gagged with a ratty old cloth.

"Oh, they look so sad," said Claire.

Evan chimed, "And can you imagine having that dirty sock looking thingy in your mouth? Yuck."

"The picture is changing," said Sigurd, pointing his finger toward the locket.

Suddenly, more of the room could be seen. The view pulled back farther and out an open window. The image panned up and down the tower before snapping back to

Claire.

"Whoa, that was intense," said Evan, stepping away from the locket. "So, we'll just have to zip to the tower and rescue them."

"It will not be as easy as that. Giants might not be very bright, but they are good hunters. They will most likely have set traps." Sigurd paused, looking toward the rickety tower. "I will distract the giants. You two find the imps and bring them back here."

"Sigurd, what about you? Evan and I can't leave you behind," said Claire, sounding genuinely concerned.

"I will be fine. Your brother can return for me after you are safe."

"You must be the bravest guy I've ever met," said Claire with a sigh. She then placed her hand on Sigurd's muscular arm. "I'll go with you. I can distract giants too. Besides, it will be easier for Evan to return here with only two passengers. He would probably struggle with three."

"Hey, I would not," shouted Evan, and Claire looked at him as if he were clueless.

"Evan, trust me. It would be too much for you to carry three of us at the same time. After you drop the imps off here, you can return for us."

Evan sighed, "Fine. Let's go."

"One more second," Claire announced before kneeling to the ground. Using her hands, she molded an object. "Here," she said while handing Evan a small dagger. "I can't have my little brother go in there completely unarmed."

"Thanks," said Evan, studying the sharp gray blade.

"You molded a dagger from rock," Sigurd marveled, his expression returning to complete adoration.

"Something like that," said Claire, looking down and playing with her hair. "I mean, I had to melt it down first. You know, to give it strength."

"Amazing," Sigurd said with a gleam in his eyes.

CHAPTER TWELVE

SNEAKER THIEF

SUDDENLY, THERE WAS A TREMENDOUS growl. Sigurd pulled out his sword, and Claire jumped behind him with her hand clenched to her chest.

"I'm hungry," said Evan, feeling his cheeks burn red.

"Here," offered Sigurd, handing Evan something wrapped in brown cloth. Evan grabbed the rectangular-shaped object, and then Sigurd handed another bar to Claire. "You will also need to keep up your strength."

"Thanks!" she squealed. "I'm starving."

Feeling anticipation much like on the morning of his birthday, Evan unwrapped the strange fabric from around his treat. This was a true gift, and he appreciated it more than words could express. Inside was a handmade granola bar with bits of nuts, oats, and raisins. The first bite tasted like heaven, even if it was difficult to sink his teeth through and the texture was hard and dry. And although the inside of his mouth hurt and his gums were probably bleeding, he ate the entire bar, thankful to ease the turbulence in his rumbling stomach. At last bite, he was ready to rescue imps.

Claire hadn't eaten her bar yet, and Evan was feeling anxious. He opened his mouth to ask her to hurry up, but the sound that emerged from it was, "Arrrough-arf-arf, whooow. Bark-bark."

Not one single intelligible word came out. Evan clasps his hands over his mouth and looked at Sigurd.

Sigurd laughed and smiled in his annoyingly charming way. "I am sorry, my friend. I had forgotten about the effect this Woofout Bar can have if you are not used to it."

"Woof-arf-uff," said Evan, still struggling to speak like a human.

Claire was quick to chime, "Wait a minute. So, if I eat this bar, then I will bark like a dog?"

"I am afraid so. But the effect only lasts for a short while."

"Arf-arf! Rrrr-uff!" Evan was really frustrated, now.

In between fits of laughter, Claire said, "I think, hee hee, he wants to know if his nose is going to stretch and ears grow long."

Evan tried to tell his sister just what he thought of her funny little comment, but all that came out was, "Whoo-hoo-woooh. Uff!"

"Thanks, Evan. But I already know how much you adore me," said Claire, chuckling some more.

"Evan, I promise you will return to normal—very soon. Just stay calm," said Sigurd.

"So, does this happen to you every time you eat one of these?" Claire asked.

"No, the bark from the Dawgbark tree has no effect on me now."

"What's a Dawgbark tree?"

"It is a rare tree, found only in Asgard. Very little is used in the Woofout Bar, but needless to say, it is extremely potent."

"Well, I'll just have to eat my bar before I go to sleep tonight. I don't want to sound like Evan."

"Rrrrr-ruff!" growled Evan, running his hand over his

throat.

"Sorry, Evan. But you have to admit you sound pretty hysterical," said Claire. "Sigurd, do you have extras of these. I'd love to play a few tricks on my friends back home."

"I do have extras, but the effect will not work in Terra. Remember, humans cannot see nor hear magic from any of Sagaas' realms."

"Darn, that would have been a great prank," said Claire. "Well, Evan, are you ready to fly?"

"Ruff!"

"I think he just said he was ready to go," said Claire. "Right, boy, or does doggy want a treat?"

"Grrrr!"

Sigurd interrupted, "I believe he just informed you that he will bite you if you do not stop teasing him."

"Fine. Let's get this rescue business over with," said Claire, looping her arm through Evan's. "At least I don't have to hold onto your tail—I know, I did it again. Sorry, sorry. I won't say anything else about your 'condition'."

Somewhat camouflaged by the starlit sky, Evan and his two companions rocketed over the labyrinth. Light from orange torches bounced off walls in the courtyard, making it easier for Evan to see. Pretty soon, he could easily hear the sounds of angry giants arguing about how to catch those pesky kids. And, unfortunately, he was flying closer and closer to them.

"Hey, that giant just called me a kid," hissed Evan.

"Evan, they're just big dumb giants. What do they know?" Claire whispered. "Hey, the Woofout bar must have worn off."

"Yeah, I guess it did," said Evan.

"This is it. Evan, you know what to do," said Sigurd, standing between Evan and Claire, his arms casually draped over both of their shoulders.

"I'll be back for you. I promise," said Evan to his sister

before climbing the tower.

Evan crawled effortlessly up the chiseled surface. In fact, his fingertips barely even scraped the stone. He slithered around many windows, peering into each one. Although, the locket had shown the imps location as up high, he wanted to make sure no giants lurked in the shadows. When he reached the top, he spied two shapes that looked like Dunkle and Barfel. But the room was black, making it difficult to tell.

A tremendous growl came from somewhere below, and Evan looked down. On the ground below him, he could see his sister and Sigurd. It was just the two of them, keeping lookout. Evan searched, but couldn't figure out what had made that noise. Suddenly, a hatch hidden under the dirt-covered ground, flung open! What came out was truly shocking. At least eight mini polar bears charged Sigurd and Claire!

"Those must be the giants' idea of 'hounds'!" yelled Claire, backing toward Sigurd.

Claire and Sigurd were surrounded by furry, white bears. They looked like baby cubs. If his sister hadn't been in immediate danger, Evan would have found the polar bears sort of cute.

And then, giants began to pour in like cockroaches. Claire pointed her finger toward the ground and spun around in a circle. Dirt beneath her and Sigurd's feet swirled around and around. Two circular pillars shot upward, lifting Claire and Sigurd up high above the fleet of white bears and fierce giants. Sigurd used a slingshot to pelt bits of rock at his enemies below. Claire extended her right hand and flexed her fingers; spikes shot up, trapping a few of the giants inside.

Polar bears tried to scramble up the pillars, digging in their sharp, black claws. But it was no use; each time one would climb a few feet, it slid right back down. One of the giants threw his club at Sigurd and knocked the hero to the ground. He tumbled down, but still managed to land on his feet. He used his sword to deflect an axe and broke its handle into shards.

"Impressive," whispered Evan. He sighed and began to turn back toward the room. When suddenly, a garbled sound came from behind him, and a bag dropped over his head and down to his sneakers! Total darkness! Evan clawed at the burlap, first with his fingers, then with his mind. He tried to use his powers to lift the bag, but this giant was too strong.

"Help!" shouted Evan, but he was jabbed by what felt like a huge finger.

"You be quiet! No yell. You not be saved," said the giant. Evan thought it sounded like the giant had a mouth full of marbles.

The space was cramped and breathing was difficult. Warm air surrounded Evan's head. He had to get out. Hopefully, Sigurd and Claire had been able to escape unharmed.

A thunderous *BOOM* erupted each time the giant's mighty feet hit the floor. The bag swung back and forth and Evan thought he was going to be sick.

"Lars, where girl?" garbled Marblemouth.

Evan strained to decipher what came from a distant giant as all he could hear were some grunts and groans.

Then Marblemouth asked, "We be only giants left? Where rest of 'em?"

Evan could hear more grumbling from the other giant, Lars.

"Stuck in stone? Ugh, I go free 'em," said Marblemouth, lifting the bag before dropping it hard on the ground. "We gots boy, now gets girl."

Without thinking, Evan shouted, "Ouch! Be a little more careful; there's precious cargo in here!" Another hurtful jab pushed into Evan's side.

"Quiet!" yelled Marblemouth.

Evan stopped squirming. He sat back and sighed. At least he had just heard that his sister and Sigurd managed to get away.

"Boy go to dungeon wit dem imps," ordered Marblemouth. "An' Lars, no you sleep."

The bag was lifted and heaved over Lars' shoulder. Evan crashed against what must have been the giant's broad back. Something small and sharp pressed into Evan's side. It didn't take long for him to remember what it was. The dagger! He struggled to move his hand, but it was difficult with all of the bouncing and squeezing of the bag. At last, he managed to free the dagger and sliced through the burlap. Unfortunately, the hole was too little for him to slip out. But through the opening, he was able to pick up a familiar odor: imps.

"Yuck," Evan grumbled, and then called out, "Dunkle, Barfel!" But all he could hear was some scuffling. "They're probably gagged," he murmured to himself.

The bag tore open, and Evan dropped hard on the stone floor. "Aahh!" he cried. His shoulder throbbed with intense pain. The giant then grabbed Evan's sneakers and yanked them right off his feet!

"Har, har, har!" laughed the nasty giant. "You go there."

"Hey, give me back my shoes!" yelled Evan.

"Me keeps 'em. Put on belt, next to human heads."

"Fine, whatever you say." Evan winced as searing pain shot from his shoulder down his arm. He spied a wobbly stool in a corner and managed to hobble over. When he attempted to sit, it tipped, and Evan fell again. The giant roared with more laughter.

"Har, har, har!" roared Lars. "I be out there."

The giant walked out, slamming shut the thick wooden door.

"Good riddance," said Evan.

Pain grew in his shoulder, and he grasped at it with

his other hand. He didn't bother to get up and stayed on his side, trying to lessen the ache. A familiar sound came from the dark corner. Evan knew the scratch and scuffle of imp toenails when he heard them. Out of blackness, two imps slid their feet in his direction. Just as Evan had assumed, they were gagged and tied to each other, back to back. Dunkle mumbled something and motioned behind him.

"I can't move my arm," Evan whined.

Dunkle shook his head and then widened his eyes before motioning toward his bound wrists.

"I don't understand. Sorry, but I need to rest," said Evan, closing his eyes. Just then, an idea occurred to him. "Oh, I can use my powers to untie you." And Dunkle sighed.

Evan concentrated and imagined removing the gag first, then untying the ropes.

"I'm free! I'm free!" Barfel cheered, waving his long arms.

"Shh, you don't want the giants to hear you," said Evan firmly. "Besides, we're stuck in this prison, and I think I dislocated my shoulder."

Dunkle and Barfel rushed to Evan's side. Staring at Evan's shoulder, Barfel exclaimed, "Use power! Use power!"

Evan couldn't believe he hadn't considered trying that before. With his eyes closed, he imagined the inside of his shoulder, underneath muscle, down to the bone. He tried to set the shoulder back into the socket. He felt a pop followed by instant relief.

"Who knew Biology class could come in handy? I amaze myself," said Evan, carefully rolling his shoulder in a circle. "It's still sore, but I'll manage."

CHAPTER THIRTEEN

FRENZY OF FUR

A SOFT HUM VIBRATED OFF THE dungeon walls. Evan shifted around, alarmed.

"Evan, Evan, this is Claire. Evan, can you hear me?"

"Claire, where are you?" Evan asked excitedly.

"Great, I've finally figured out how to work this locket," said Claire.

"What? Where are you?" Evan rushed around, but there were no windows and the only door was shut. "Is there a secret tunnel or something? I can't see you."

"Evan, listen, I'm not sure how long this will work," said Claire. "Sigurd and I managed to trap a lot of the giants, but more kept coming. We needed to rest, so we hid in the labyrinth."

"How can I hear you?" Evan asked.

"Not only does the locket show us what we ask to see, but it also works like a cell phone."

"I'm afraid it didn't work so great at seeing the future, fifty-eight minutes or whatever. Dunkle and Barfel weren't up in the tower," Evan sighed. "Sigurd was right, it was a trap."

"The locket worked fine. We didn't ask the right

question," Claire corrected. "Most likely the imps were in the tower. The giants must have moved them before we arrived."

"Yeah, they were probably moved down to this medieval looking dungeon. So, we should have asked where they would be in the future," Evan realized. "That information would have been great two hours ago."

"Look, I'm learning how to use the divining locket as we go," said Claire, sounding irritated. "We'll get you out of there. Just hang tight."

The room filled with light, and then returned to darkness.

"Claire, Claire. I guess time was up," said Evan, searching for his sister's lost voice. He stood beside a wall and ran his fingers around a cluster of stones. "Dunkle, Barfel—we need to get out of here. Do either of you know where we are?"

"Let me see," said Dunkle, his fingers stroking his chin thoughtfully. "We came from the hall on the other side of that door."

"I already gathered that," said Evan. "Which wall leads outside?"

"This wall. Yes, yes this one," Barfel chimed, pointing off to his left.

"Dunkle, do you agree with Barfel? Lars the giant will most likely hear us break out. So, we have only one shot at this," said Evan.

Dunkle shrugged his shoulders. "I would listen to Barfel. He is usually right about such things."

"You're sure you believe him?" Evan asked, looking over to where the red imp was hugging the mildew-stained wall. Dunkle nodded enthusiastically and, although reluctant, Evan agreed. "That will have to be good enough."

Using his finger as a guide, Evan outlined the shape of a rectangle. As he drew imaginary lines, stones rattled and shifted apart. Cracks appeared and then stretched. Stones crumbled and, for good measure, Evan slammed them against the wooden door. Large fists pounded on the other side, and Lars's anger could be heard in his voice. Evan wasn't sure what Lars was saying and hoped to never find out.

Barfel leapt over to the hole, and then hopped through. Dunkle was quick to follow. Evan was about to dash over when he stopped and looked back at the door. The barricade of stones started to budge, and the giant's head popped into view.

"Stop!" shouted Lars.

"I am so outta here," said Evan, rushing behind Dunkle.

"Back! Back!" roared Lars.

Evan and the two imps now stood on the outside of the fort in the dried up moat. The labyrinth wasn't very far. Evan judged the distance and had to make a decision: his sister or the imps?

"For now, Claire's safe with Sigurd. Imps, we need to hurry," said Evan, reaching for them. "Grab hold of my hands."

Dunkle and Barfel didn't ask questions, they scurried over and clung to Evan. The imps' long nails dug into his hands and both of their heads buried into Evan's legs.

"All right guys, you're inflicting a lot of pain. Can you ease back? I need to be able to concentrate while I search for Claire," said Evan, and the imps loosened their grip a little. "And whatever you do, don't look down."

Evan felt rather accomplished as his flying skills had clearly improved. With relative ease, he shot through the sky while surveying below. But Claire was nowhere in sight.

As soon as their feet touched the ground, Evan instructed, "I need to go back. Stay right here. I shouldn't be too long. Oh, and stay away from the cave. There's a dragon in there. But don't worry." He leapt up and zipped back toward the labyrinth.

Evan searched for his sister, guessing she would be surrounded by metal ivy. Most of the labyrinth still flourished with green vines, and Evan was getting frustrated. That was until he finally spotted a trail of brown metal and heard the sound of battle armor clanking together. Some of the labyrinth's green walls shook, transforming instantly into sharp barbed wire and spades.

"Please be Claire," he whispered and dove closer into the labyrinth, careful not to touch the walls.

Chains rattled and swords clanked. And was that Claire? She must have been battling ten or more giants. Odd, she didn't look frightened. Was she actually enjoying herself? Just as he suspected, there were at least ten giants doing their utmost to capture Claire and Sigurd. Sigurd battled two and three giants at once. His sword flashed with speed and efficiency. Sigurd knocked down the slow and clumsy giants, preparing them for Claire's stone and dirt prisons. Within a matter of minutes, most of the giants were trapped in strange-looking cocoons. But more could be heard a few yards away. And mini polar bears circled around Sigurd and Claire, snarling and snapping at them.

One bear leapt and knocked Claire to the ground! While it might have been the size of a large dog, its teeth were much bigger. Just then, five more giants turned the corner.

"Heel!" shouted one of the giants, and the bear sat back. "Must keep girl 'live."

Another giant threw a piece of red meat, and the bear jumped off Claire, attacking his reward with a vengeance.

A giant hollered to Sigurd, "Weapon down!" and pointed a long spear right for Claire's throat. "Slice her, I will."

Sigurd looked at Claire's frightened face and laid down his sword.

"Sigurd, keep fighting!" shouted Claire.

"Now, you stand," said the giant, pointing his spear toward Claire. She sighed and sat upright, when suddenly, her left foot was pulled off the ground!

"Hey, where you go?"

Her body flipped upside down and her hair dangled toward the ground. She thrashed, swinging her arms. Evan learned a few new words as they hurled from her mouth.

"Claire, how are you—" began Sigurd, but then he too was swept up. Evan managed to lift Sigurd by both feet. But he too was upside down and the polar bears bat his head a few times with their paws. Evan raised himself higher, and once Claire and Sigurd were beyond reach of the giants' massive clubs and bounding polar bears, Evan pulled Claire and Sigurd over to where he hovered.

"Claire!" shouted Evan.

"Evan, flip me over!" cried out Claire.

"I'm not so sure if I can," said Evan, but in truth, he knew if he tried hard enough, he could. "I didn't even know I could make you fly without touching you. I thought I would have to hold onto you to make you fly. With all of the giants coming, I panicked. I tried to figure out how to reach you and wished for you to fly. And then up you went."

"I guess that would only make sense. I mean, you can move other objects around without touching them," Claire rationalized.

"We better hurry out of here, it is only a matter of time before those giants figure out how to throw their clubs at us," said Sigurd, staring at the ugly faces beneath him.

"Yeah, and I'm feeling dizzy. Make sure you fly high enough so my face doesn't whack into a tree or something," said Claire.

"Right, good point," said Evan. "You know, you don't look so good."

"You think? I'm hanging upside down here," said a green-faced Claire.

~~~☙❧~~~

An orange glow illuminated off the cliff, lighting the way, as if Evan were a ship lost at sea. The imps must have built a fire. He looked over at Sigurd and Claire, and decided it was time to turn them upright. Evan rotated both his hands as if he were turning the steering wheel of a car. Claire and Sigurd spun around in a few cartwheels before settling.

"Thanks," said Claire.

"No prob. I guess I could have flipped you earlier, after all. Funny thing, huh?" said Evan.

"Not really; just get us back to the cliff. I want to stand on my own again," said Claire.

They approached the mountain. Dunkle and Barfel leapt up and down upon seeing them, looping their arms through each other's and doing a little square dance.

"Hurray! Hurray!" sang Barfel.

"I am afraid we are not yet safe," Sigurd explained. "Those giants will continue to hunt for us. And there are more giants in the caves. They will keep searching, and by morning, these lands will be swarming with them."

"We better head out," Evan announced.

"I would consider it an honor if you would allow me to accompany you on your quest," Sigurd offered.

"Sigurd, thanks for helping us, but we can't expect you to drop what you're doing, capturing dragons and all. Besides, you could end up dying," said Evan. "This is a very dangerous quest."

"I realize what is at risk. Claire explained everything to me. From what I understand, if you fail, everyone will be affected," said Sigurd, packing up his remaining gear.

"But—" began Evan.

"I insist," Sigurd interrupted, without looking up.

"There's not enough room on our boat."

"That is not a problem. We can take my boat. It is just a few miles away."

"Maybe I don't want to take your boat. I like our boat."

"I have little doubt your boat is fine, but my ship is already stocked with all of the supplies we will need."

"With stuff like those barking-dog treats? No thank you. Besides, we have supplies, and if we need something we can just make it."

"What about food and fresh water? Do you have those things too? Besides, you do not even have shoes to wear," said Sigurd. Evan reached for his rumbling stomach and looked down at his bare feet.

"I am hungry. And I did have sneakers, but that giant took them!"

"A giant took your shoes?" Claire asked. "Why? It's not like they'd fit a giant's foot."

"I think he wanted them as a trophy or something," said Evan.

"How weird," said Claire.

"Evan, you need to trust me. My ship will serve us better. And I assure you, I am not here to take over. You can still be Captain Evan," Sigurd added with a little smile.

Evan glared over at Claire. "You told him to call me Captain Evan?"

"Get over it," Claire said and approached Sigurd. "Thanks for helping us. I'm not sure how we can ever repay you."

"Beautiful heroine, your bright smile is all the payment I need," said Sigurd, brushing his fingertip along her cheek.

"Dude, that's my sister. Do you mind?" declared

Evan.

"What, Evan...uh," stammered Claire. "Sigurd, don't listen to him."

"Whatever," said Evan, rolling his eyes.

"What about the dragon, Bergkonge?" Claire asked Sigurd, as if trying to change the subject.

Sigurd contemplated something before saying, "This might sound crazy, but as soon as we are far enough away, I need for you and Evan to reopen the cave."

"But that will set him free!" she said, eyes wide.

Sigurd grinned somewhat fiendishly. "Bergkonge could end up distracting a few giants for us."

With a deep gulp of air, Evan lifted the group up into the sky. The long night had finally come to an end, and the morning sun rose in the east. They sped toward Sigurd's boat, and Claire looked down at the cave. From a distance, she broke apart the wall of dirt and stones. Quickly, Evan swiped away the fallen rubble with his powers. It didn't take long for Bergkonge to emerge, fire surging from his open mouth. He stalked around, sniffing the ground.

Bergkonge's massive wings thrust down. Leaves and dirt spun like a cyclone around the dragon. He leapt a few yards above ground, rushed toward the edge of the cliff, and soared toward the tower. Evan cringed as he imagined the giants' surprise at running into Bergkonge.

CHAPTER FOURTEEN

STUCK WITH BULL SHARKS

SIGURD'S SHIP CAME INTO VIEW, and Evan couldn't help but marvel. It was larger than Evan's glass ship, with a mightier mast and a fiercer dragon carved on its bow.

"How are you able to sail this ship all by yourself?" Evan asked, scowling.

"It was given to me by the gods. It is made from enchanted wood and sails itself," Sigurd said nonchalantly.

"Why did the gods give you an enchanted ship?"

"They wanted to show me their gratitude for capturing so many pesky dragons. Besides, they realized the mightier my ship, the easier it would be to do my job."

As soon as their feet touched the deck, Sigurd rushed to the helm, and Dunkle followed. Evan sighed, realizing his days as "captain" were officially over.

"Evan, we could use your help," Sigurd yelled the length of the ship, and Evan hurried to join them.

"Claire told me how you raced your boat through the rocks," said Sigurd. "After we chart our new course, do you think you could quicken our pace to Hlesey?"

"I suppose so," Evan responded. "Remind me again;

97

what exactly is Hlesey?"

"It is an island that rests above the Undersea Hall of Aegir and Ran," said Sigurd.

"Don't you think Aegir will have guards protecting the entrance?" said Evan. "If he's determined to use the Serpent's Ring to unlock Jormundgand, then he's going to try to keep us away."

"Good point," said Sigurd, rubbing his hand over his chin. "We will just have to figure out another way through. For now, steer us in that direction. I will be back after Dunkle and I review the map."

"I'll help," said Claire, rushing toward Sigurd.

Evan looked at Barfel and sighed, "I guess it's just you and me."

"Quite right!" declared Barfel, leaping up onto a wooden platform. He placed his hand over his eyes and scanned the horizon. "Up the mast I go! Better to see! Better to see!"

He climbed gracefully up the pole, much like a monkey. Evan was left alone to man the ship. He wished he had his pirate hat to complete the effect. It had been left behind, on his glass Viking ship. The more he thought about it, the more irritated he became. Why should they have to use Sigurd's ship, anyway? What's wrong with their ship? Besides, his hat was woven from thread off his favorite baseball cap. He wanted it back.

All of a sudden, something flew toward him. It was his pirate hat! It spun through the air, whizzing in his direction, before landing right on his head.

"Did I do that?" Evan wondered. But it didn't really matter; he had gotten what he wanted.

Water splattered against the bow, and the boat rocked. Evan focused, pushing against the strong current. He lifted the ship a little and was able to speed forward. Staring straight, he aimed cautiously and carefully toward Hlesey. This time, he wouldn't overshoot his destination.

Sigurd stepped out of the cabin, Claire and Dunkle close at his heels. He turned toward the bow and his hair was tussled by the wind.

"Blondielocks," mumbled Evan. For the first time, he knew what Sigurd and Claire had in common. He imagined they would spend their time together staring at themselves in a mirror, while brushing their hair.

"This ship has never before seen this speed," Sigurd announced and peered over the side. "We are not touching the water. How do you manage this?" Sigurd shook his head as he approached, his hair still flowing with the breeze. After reaching Evan, he rested his hand on the boy's shoulder. "You are tired and need to rest. I can see it in your eyes."

Evan continued to stare ahead, concentrating. "I can't rest. If I do, the sea will push us back."

"You did not sleep last night and are going to exhaust yourself. It is crucial you have strength and mental clarity when you meet with Aegir," said Sigurd.

Evan agreed. He returned the ship to water and released his hold. But just as he did, waves shaped like giant hands reached up and grabbed the vessel.

"Aegir must have set the ocean against us. I am afraid I did not take that into consideration. I am sorry for allowing this to happen," said Sigurd.

"This isn't your fault. There has to be something we can do," said Claire, determination hot in her voice. "What about the locket? Look, it's already glowing; we can use it."

Evan and Sigurd rushed to her side. Claire opened the locket and all three stared in. Colorful beams came into view. "I haven't asked anything yet," whispered Claire.

"It wants to show us something," said Sigurd, his arm dropping casually to her waist.

Evan tried to pay attention to the locket, but felt irritated at Sigurd's blatant display. After all, this guy just met Claire, and she was his sister. She was annoying and a big royal pain most of the time, but in a small way, Evan felt protective. Who was this Sigurd, anyway? He probably had a million other girlfriends, and Claire was going to be hurt. And Evan would be left having to listen to his sister's endless wailing and crying. He was certain it would get annoying, fast.

"That's us!" exclaimed Claire, forcing Evan's attention back to the locket.

Sure enough, on deck stood Evan, Claire, Sigurd, Dunkle, and Barfel, they could be seen from overhead. Colorful sharks gathered and knocked into the ship. The view shifted, and Evan was yanked underwater by a large net. He fought, pulling against golden ropes.

"It is Ran's net," said Sigurd, still staring at the oval mirror. "She must have her sights set on capturing Evan. She enjoys using her golden net to catch sailors. She then takes them to the Undersea Hall, forcing them to admire and worship her forever."

The scene shifted again. There was a sudden flash of violet.

"The net's empty! Evan's gone! Where did he go?" yelled Claire, shaking the golden locket, but she was disrupted by tremendous pounding against the boat's underside.

Water tightened its hold on the ship. It was hit again and again, with more thumping and banging. Wood split and water spurted through.

"Aegir's trying to sink us!" shrilled Dunkle, circling madly around the deck.

"Not today," said Evan, trying to sound calm.

Sharks rammed the boat. Its sides splintered and shattered. Claire waved her hands over the shredded wood and sealed it back together.

"The boat's breaking apart! I'm not sure I can hold it

together for long!" screamed Claire, frantically mending the boards.

The sharks multiplied, and Evan tried to mentally push them away. To his surprise he was able to slow their movements. That was until they became still, frozen in place. Not even a tail swished. As Evan focused below, he neglected the other side of the ship. And *wham!* another shark struck from the opposite direction. Evan was tossed overboard, right into the midst of several immobile sharks!

With all of his strength, he tried to rise out of the water. But something strange happened. The water changed and molded to his body. He tried to kick, but his legs were caught in the gelatinous substance. The only part of his body still above the surface was his head.

"Evan, we'll get you," shouted Claire, peering over the ship's side.

"You can't come in this water! It's like jelly. You won't be able to get back out," yelled Evan.

"I will throw you a rope," hollered Sigurd, swinging a lariat. He released its looped end toward Evan, who wasn't able to even squirm.

"It's no use! I can't move my arms!" cried out Evan.

"Then I will come down," said Sigurd, edging over the side.

"No, you need to protect the ship," declared Evan.

"The sharks are as stuck as you are. The water surrounding us has turned to glue," said Claire.

Close to Evan, jelly-water oozed together, forming into a rounded shape. A face molded into the clear mass, and a man with a long beard and wavy hair surfaced. Life came to his eyes, and he spoke in a waterlogged voice, "I know what you are after, and you cannot have it."

"Are you Aegir?" Evan asked to the talking ball of water.

"I am Aegir, god and protector of the sea. You must return home, and no harm will come to you. If you decide foolishly to stay, I might not be so generous."

"If I return home, I will drown along with the rest of the planet," said Evan. "The way I see it, I have no other choice. But you do. You don't have to drown everyone on land. We can work out something, can't we?"

"The decision has been made. It is only a short matter of time before the Serpent's Ring unlocks Jormundgand."

"Then my decision has been made too. I'm going to stop you, no matter what it takes."

"So be it. You have chosen poorly, boy." Aegir dissolved back into the sea.

Evan looked up and noticed Claire's eyes had widened. "Evan, look behind you!"

A golden net emerged and landed over Evan's head. Just as the divining locket predicted, he was dragged under. He tugged, but the woven fiber didn't relent. It pulled him down, deeper and deeper into the ocean.

"At least my sister's safe," said Evan, letting out his reserve of air. He felt his chest collapse, forcing him to inhale. Surprisingly, he could breathe in the jelly-water. He wasn't going to drown.

Down, down, down he went. Up above, frozen sharks and the intact ship remained still. The water's surface became a pale haze, far away. Before long, Evan was surrounded by darkness, but fluorescent lights appeared as pinpoints deep in the abyss. Evan was certain that was where he was going. It was probably the Undersea Hall of Aegir and Ran.

Evan was doomed; he was certain of it. When, all of a sudden, Evan and the net began to spin in circles. Around and around, until the net fell open and sunk toward the ocean floor. He was released, but the water was still too thick for him to swim. He tried a climbing motion, but his arms and legs were trapped. A large tail swished by, and a mass of violet hair swooped across his face.

CHAPTER FIFTEEN

WAY OF THE MERMAID

WITH ONE ARM CIRCLING EVAN'S chest, she sped through the water. He could feel the movement of her body, as she guided them toward pinpoints of fluorescent light. It was over for Evan. He knew he was in the clutches of Ran. Pretty soon, Aegir would serve Evan as a snack to the sea serpent, Jormundgand.

They raced at an incredible speed, tearing through water—right for the tiny lights. But to Evan's surprise, she shifted direction and the colorful lights disappeared. Although Evan wanted to see where he was being taken, he squeezed his eyes shut. He could still feel her delicate fingers and long hair as it billowed around, whipping his back.

The water began to change. It felt cooler, like it had thinned. It felt like seawater was supposed to. The jellywater fell away from his body, leaving only a little around his face. At least for the time being, he could breathe. But as it melted, Evan began to worry.

Their pace slowed, and his eyes reopened. They were heading toward a large dome. Evan probably wouldn't have realized it was there, if it hadn't been for his image

103

being reflected on its surface. The reflection showed his captor was not a woman, nor a goddess. She was a mermaid! She was the most incredible looking creature he had ever seen. Jewels were embedded along her tail in intricate designs and continued to trace along her body like a dress. Her purple hair shimmered and sparkled, and Evan was breathless—literally, breathless.

As they approached the dome, their reflections continued to enlarge. Surely, she would stop before slamming into it. But she didn't; she flicked her tail and propelled faster! To his amazement, they slid through the dome with relative ease. Millions of tiny bubbles popped along his skin, tingling. One bubble attached itself to Evan's mouth and extended down his throat. He could breathe normally again.

"I'm definitely not in Michigan anymore," he said to himself as they entered the dome full of thick goo and natural seawater. Evan could only kind of walk and felt a little silly moving along like Frankenstein's monster.

Up ahead, an underwater city glistened. Merpeople and tropical fish moved around buildings molded from glass. Each colorful structure stemmed from the ground, blending together—yellow, green, purple, red, and every other color imaginable. It was like staring at rainbow popsicles, twisting around as they tapered up to a point.

"What is this Michigan? Is it another realm?" an enchanting voice flowed toward Evan.

Evan turned his head toward his mermaid captor. She too wore a bubble over her mouth and down to her throat. She was staring into his eyes, studying him.

"Michigan is nothing like this place. Much more normal," he said.

"This is normal," she said, gliding her arm through the water as she motioned toward the city.

"For you, maybe, but this is far from normal for me. My name is Evan."

"I know who you are, Evan Jones," she said, and as she spoke, each word sounded like music.

"I suppose you're going to take me to Aegir."

"Why would I do that? It would not have made sense to go through the trouble of rescuing you from Ran's net if that were my intention."

"I don't understand. You rescued me? You're one of the good guys?"

"Dear boy, Aegir is not a 'bad guy.' He believes what he is doing is best for all creatures of the sea. Unfortunately, he has lost his sympathy for the beings that dwell on land," said the mermaid with wisdom beyond her years. Evan guessed her age at sixteen, tops.

"First of all, I'm not a boy," Evan corrected. "And, I have to disagree about Aegir. Come on, anyone willing to flood the entire planet has to be evil."

"He is coming from a different perspective, an ancient perspective. Remember, he is very old and has seen many evils occur on land."

"So, he thinks he should kill everybody and start over?"

"Yes."

"Well, that guy's nuts. And you seem to understand him pretty well. How can I be so sure you aren't working for him and this isn't some sort of trap?"

"The merpeople have been friends with Aegir for thousands of years. It is only recently our paths have split. Although we too are upset with mankind for polluting our homes, we do not believe washing the planet is the answer. We believe in the innovation and creativity of land people to correct their own mistakes."

"I'm glad you are on my side. I just can't believe you were friends with Aegir."

"Good friends," she said, turning away. "My best friend is one of his daughters, Himinglaeva. We haven't spoken for a long time."

105

"Aegir has daughters?"

"Yes, nine of them, each one is a wave. My name is Lazonia. I need to take you to the council."

"The council? Why do I need to—" began Evan before being taken hold of by Lazonia and then whizzed through water like a torpedo. She darted effortlessly between merpeople and fish, flipping and swishing her tail. Evan noticed the other merpeople did not have bubbles attached to their faces, and he wondered why.

She swam up and along the side of a towering building. And as soon as they reached the top, she slid onto a balcony. Evan kneeled over and hugged the shiny floor. He could barely see through the rose-colored glass, but he guessed he must have been at least twenty stories high.

"Father!" declared Lazonia as she streamed across the room.

Edging closer to the open doorway, Evan peeked inside. Lazonia was hugging an older merman who had a short, light-blue beard. A strange sound came from the older merman. Lazonia screeched something and motioned toward Evan. The merman formed a large bubble around his mouth and throat.

"My dear daughter, you have succeeded in your task," said the merman, radiating energy and wisdom. "I knew you would."

There were other mermen and mermaids in the room. They floated in a circle. A unique symbol was beneath each council member. At least, Evan hoped these were council members and not prison guards, ready to take him away.

Etched beneath Lazonia's father was an image of a sea serpent, not Jormundgand, but a serpent nonetheless.

"So this is Evan Jones," said the merman, "the very same boy after which Aegir has sent his entire army?" Lazonia nodded and glanced toward Evan, giving him a reassuring smile. The merman continued, "Boy, do not be afraid. You will be safe here. My name is Ragnar. I am head of this council and father of Lazonia. It is also my duty to watch over the seas' many creatures and serpents, including Jormundgand. From what I understand, he might soon be released. We must not let that happen," Ragnar said with an edge to his voice. "Come and stand in the center of our circle."

"I am sorry for interrupting your meeting. I'll be fine over here," said Evan, shying away.

"This meeting is about you. Whether you like it or not, you are a part of this story. Please, join us."

Evan shuffled toward the center of the room, and a brilliant-orange beam glowed beneath the floor. Light shot up and then poured out. A screeching sound occurred that reminded him of nails over a chalkboard, making him wince. Something was scratching right under Evan's bare feet!

Light diminished, and Evan's body began to float. He hovered above the new etching. Quiet ramblings and astonished gasps ensued. After lifting one eyelid, Evan wished he hadn't.

"Why is everyone staring at me like that?" he wondered.

Lazonia, who seemed to force a smile, pointed toward the floor. Etched into the glass below was the image of Jormundgand. The serpent was circling around to bite its tail. Suddenly, the image came to life and started to move. A small golden ring floated toward Jormundgand's collar and attached itself inside a tiny recess. Jormundgand's mouth opened, and his tail was set free! A current of ripples waved over and the image vanished.

"It would appear Odin has something big planned for you, my boy," said Ragnar. "We had better get started."

CHAPTER SIXTEEN

WOODEN SHARK-PODS

"WHAT DOES THAT MEAN, EXACTLY?" cried out Evan.

A mermaid with long silver hair made a chiming sound, but Evan couldn't understand her.

"Remember council members, humans do not understand our language," announced Ragnar. "You will need to form a membrane around your mouth and throat so he can understand you." Bubbles formed over the mouth and throat of every merperson there.

The mermaid with silver hair then regarded Evan. "Your symbol shows what you will face, and what could happen if you fail. If you succeed, then your symbol will complete itself and remain here permanently."

"But, what if I fail?" Evan asked; his voice shaky.

A merman with a crimson-colored beard interrupted, "Then your failure will be etched into the glass. Of course, we will be here to see it. You, however, will not be."

"That is quite enough," declared the silver-haired merlady. "Can you not see that he is already frightened?"

"As well he should be," shouted Redbeard.

The two bickered about the value of mankind, and whether or not it was such a good idea to turn against

Aegir. After all, what has mankind ever done for them except spoil their oceans and refuse to share land? Obviously, this wasn't the council members' first argument.

"Silence!" roared Ragnar, who raised his arms. "Lazonia, please, show Evan our city. Apparently, we have some unfinished business to attend to in here."

As Redbeard proceeded to defend his stance, Evan was led through a tubular hallway. Evan could hear the outburst that followed Redbeard's argument. And then the merpeople's perfectly clear English transformed into wails and squeals.

"You must be hungry," said Lazonia, reaching for Evan's hand. "You will be able to move around easier with my help."

Still too stunned to talk, Evan reached for her hand. She swerved around multiple loops. Occasionally, the tube split. Expertly, Lazonia chose which way to go, leading him along hallways lined with many oval doorways; some were transparent, some were not. Evan wondered if any of the doors led to offices, and whether or not there were cubicles inside. He laughed a little as he imagined a fish wearing glasses, typing on a computer.

"Why are you laughing?" Lazonia asked, slowing her pace.

"Oh, nothing. I'm trying to think about something funny."

"You are an interesting creature, Evan Jones," she said and paused. She appeared to study him before continuing. "I shall introduce you to mermaid cuisine. This café happens to offer the best around," she said sweetly.

"Thanks. I'd like that," he said, remembering how little he had eaten over the last few days.

Long strands of seaweed grew up and along the walls and ceiling, coiling and looping the entire length of the hallway. At the end of each vine a cluster of underwater flowers illuminated both color and light. Up ahead, a glass archway lead to the "outdoor" café. Glass sculptures of shells and mermaids formed a wall around the terrace. High tables rested on top of a mosaic design made from glass and seashells. There were no chairs. Everyone floated in place, picking at their food and drinking from bizarre bottles.

"So that's how you drink," observed Evan.

"Did you think we drank seawater? Yuck. I happen to know what fish do in seawater." She leaned closer to whisper, "And if I were you, I would not drink it."

Evan laughed and said, "Good point."

"We drink what is equivalent to your honeysuckle. It is very sweet and comes in different colors. We harvest it ourselves and have to bottle the liquid or obviously—"

"Otherwise, it would float away," interrupted Evan.

"Yes. It might sound silly to you, but drinking from a bottle does a remarkable job of keeping saltwater out."

Lazonia pulled Evan over to a table near an open pathway. Mermaids and mermen swam between buildings, greeting each other as they traveled.

"Would you like for me to order?" Lazonia asked, and Evan's attention returned to her.

"That would be great."

A green-and-yellow striped fish approached their table. Lazonia made some sounds like "click-click, eech." The fish spun around, and swoosh, it was gone. Evan stared at her with his eyebrows still raised.

"I know you will enjoy the food," she stated.

"I'm sure I will. What language were you speaking?"

"That is how we communicate with other creatures of the sea. Every animal and fish has his own language. In fact, you should hear whales sing. It is very beautiful."

The fish returned with two glass bottles. A bottle of orange liquid landed in front of Evan and a pale blue one floated right into Lazonia's hand.

"Blap-blop, blup," said the fish, and it zipped away.

"He said our food should be here shortly," translated Lazonia. "Are you going to try your nectar?"

Evan reached for the bottle and lifted it toward his face. Carefully, he inserted it through his bubble and brought it to his mouth. It was a little embarrassing to drink nectar from a baby bottle, but he did it anyway. At first, a little seawater streamed in, and it definitely didn't taste very good. He then sealed his lips tighter and managed to pull in the juice.

"It tastes like orange soda. I had something like this at Dr. Irving's house. He said it was called Fizzy-Whizzle," exclaimed Evan. But Lazonia did not respond, she just fluttered her eyelashes and smiled behind her bottle.

The fish waiter returned, holding two platters. Covering them were protective bubbles. Fish-waiter nudged them along; they floated down and landed onto the table. He clicked again, and then swam to another group of merpeople. Evan looked for silverware, but couldn't find any. He watched as Lazonia reached inside her "food bubble." She then removed a stick resembling a French fry. After biting into it, she grinned.

Evan stared at his meal encased by a similar bubble. It looked good, but he hesitated. Again, he watched Lazonia claim another piece of food. He was amazed her food bubble didn't burst. Gently, he inserted his hand inside his bubble, pinched some food, and then brought it out.

"It didn't pop," he said with relief, and Lazonia giggled.

Although it looked like a French fry, it clearly wasn't. Evan nibbled on a small piece. It was kind of rubbery, with a lemony-fish flavor. Considering he had never been a fan of seafood, it was pretty all right.

"So, what is this? Fish or something?" Evan asked, placing another stick in his mouth.

Lazonia's eyes widened and she gasped. "No, no, no. We never eat fish! What do you think we are cannibals?"

"Sorry, I'm just not sure what this is."

"This is fried seaweed frisatta," she said, relaxing her tone.

"Well, it's good," he said, trying not to say anything else that would upset his one undersea ally. "So, what's up with the bubbles on our faces? Do they help us breathe or something?"

"Your bubble helps *you* breathe. *I* do not need one to breathe underwater."

"Why are you wearing one?"

"So I am able to communicate with you," she answered somewhat snootily. "Have you ever tried to talk underwater? It does not work very well. We merpeople do not use our mouths to speak to one another. We use our throats, making sounds much like dolphins."

For the remainder of lunch, Evan kept quiet, simply enjoying his seaweed frisatta and nectar.

∽∾∾∾

"Let's go," said Lazonia. "I want to show you our glorious city."

And with that, they were off. Lazonia led them right in the middle of other merpeople who were swimming along the avenue.

"Lazonia, everyone is staring at me. I thought merpeople were used to seeing humans," said Evan.

"Never before has a human been down to our city. Ever since Aegir practically waged war against anyone who disagrees with him, we do not leave our protective dome. It is no longer safe for us out there," answered Lazonia.

Evan tried to ignore the onlookers; instead of staring rudely back at them, he studied the many drawings and symbols etched into glass buildings.

"What are those?" Evan asked, pointing to a sign

112

hanging above an open doorway.

"Those are ancient Viking runes, similar to your alphabet. Those runes say 'Porpoises Welcome'."

"They look pretty cool. Can you teach me how to read them?"

"Sure. We can start with the basics. There is an old castle just outside the city. I shall take you there now. I have a feeling the symbols carved into the walls will fascinate you," she said, grabbing hold of his hand.

Although it made Evan queasy, he couldn't help being impressed by Lazonia's speed. In a few seconds, they must have traveled half a mile away from the city.

"Evan, come over here and look at this," she said, staring at a broken-down castle. Many pictures and runes were carved onto the stone walls. "A long time ago, these buildings were a thriving part of our world. Up until this century the merpeople built with blocks of stone. That was until we discovered how to melt down sand to form our glass structures. Merpeople used to carve pictures onto these walls. This image here tells a story about—" she began but was cut short by a loud crash.

Evan and Lazonia didn't have to travel far to see what made the commotion. On the other side of the fallen castle, two sharks were buried in the sand.

"Sharks are forbidden to swim in here. This dome is protected. How did they find us?" she said nervously and reached for Evan. "We need to leave!"

Evan moved away from her and traveled closer to the sharks. Funny thing was they looked like bull sharks, but instead of having vibrant colors on their skin, they had brown rings like a tree.

"Wait a minute. Look at that tail; it's broken off," said Evan. "And both sharks seem to be made from wood."

"Sharks made from a tree? That is impossible."

Just then, the top fin of one of the sharks lifted and out climbed Sigurd.

CHAPTER SEVENTEEN

ETCHED IN STONE

"**B**LAPA!" SHOUTED CLAIRE, AFTER LIFTING the top of the other shark. "Bla-blen-blee!"

"What did she say?" Evan said to Lazonia, who shrugged and rushed over to Claire. With the help of Lazonia, Claire's face was encapsulated within a bubble.

"Whoa, who is she? She has a tail," said Claire. "And I can breathe."

"I know. I'm not sure what this bubble thingy is, but we can breathe in it," Evan yelled while swimming toward his sister, a smile stretching his face. "How were you able to find me?"

After helping Barfel out of his shark-pod, Sigurd rushed to Claire. And although Claire pretended to need his assistance, Evan knew better. His sister had been winning trophies in gymnastics for more than eight years. He watched as Claire accidently (on purpose) fell into the arms of her hero.

Dunkle rushed to Evan's side. "Evan, you are safe! Claire's locket was not sufficiently clear about that part," declared Dunkle, his face also encompassed by a bubble.

"So, you must have figured out how to use the locket correctly," said Evan, trying to gain his sister's attention away from Sigurd.

"I was unaware Sigurd the Dragon Slayer had joined your quest. Evan, you are lucky indeed," Lazonia said, still studying the hero.

"My days of slaying dragons have been over for quite some time now," informed Sigurd, flashing his annoyingly bright smile her way. His face bubble seemed to magnify his large white teeth. Evan hurried to her side, wedging himself between Sigurd and the mermaid.

"This is Lazonia. She rescued me from Ran's net," explained Evan.

"Is Ragnar still head of the council?" Sigurd asked.

"Yes, he is," answered Lazonia. "I am certain he would like to see you again."

Sigurd looked at Claire and said, "I met Ragnar a few years ago. We had a very interesting adventure together."

"That sounds fascinating! I'd love to hear more," said Claire, wearing a silly grin.

"Listen, that's great, but I have some important things to tell you," Evan cut in. "But first, what exactly did the divining locket show you?"

"Basically, the same thing you saw. The golden net pulled you under, and the flash of violet hair," Claire said and looked at Lazonia. "I'm guessing that was you."

"Lazonia freed me from the net and brought me here. Isn't this place great! I mean, just look at the city. It's made from some kind of glass," said Evan excitedly. "And I met the council. Something strange happened when I was in the center of the room. An image appeared on the glass below me."

Sigurd added, "I have heard there is a symbol permanently etched into the floor, one for each member of council. Supposedly, the symbols magically alter along with that merperson's actions. But, I have never heard of a human having the ability to develop a symbol."

"No human has ever been to our city," explained

Lavonia. "Not only is the dome a shield, it camouflages our city, as well."

"Claire, how were you able to see the dome?" Evan asked.

"We couldn't," she answered. "The locket guided us. It was like staring at a map."

"Well, I'm impressed," said Evan, "and nice job on the shark-pod."

"The submarine was my idea, but disguising us as sharks was Sigurd's," she said and looked at her "hero" adoringly.

"Sigurd, your enchanted ship is ruined," realized Evan.

Sigurd shrugged his shoulders. "It served its purpose. Perhaps, one day, I will come by another vessel of its equal."

"Didn't you say the gods gave that one to you as a gift," Evan asked. "I doubt you'll find another ship like it, ever again."

"Life has a funny way of working itself out, often times for the better," Sigurd said optimistically.

"Over here! Over here!" shouted Barfel. He and Dunkle were standing by the ancient castle.

"The imps must have found the prophecy," said Lazonia, and then her tail swooshed, giving her speed greater than the others.

A few moments later, Evan, Claire, and Sigurd reached the wall.

"You were going to tell me something about this picture, just before they showed up," Evan said to Lazonia.

"Is that Evan?" Claire asked, placing her finger on the carved image of a boy.

"That can't be me! You said this castle was from a long time ago. I'm guessing that was before I was even born. How could that possibly be me?"

"My ancestors had great knowledge of the future. Most of their predictions have come true. Many of them were good, a few were not," said Lazonia, resting her long webbed fingers on Evan's arm.

And there was Jormundgand, taking up most of the space. As usual, the image showed him biting his tail. Except in this portrayal, he was wrapped around a carving of the world. This wall must have been enchanted because the planet spun around on its axis. A man with a shaggy beard was carved on the left side. Stretching his hand toward Jormundgand, he offered a tiny ring. Evan moved closer to study the small object. Just then, the tiny ring floated above the man's upward facing palm.

It was the Serpent's Ring, Evan was certain of it. Now the picture came together. This must have been Aegir, and he was unlocking the giant sea serpent. Evan scanned over to the other side of the image. There, standing on a cliff, was a small boy facing a massive wave. Sharks were swimming in the wave—just like in Evan's dream.

"What am I going to do?" Evan said and sank to the ocean's floor, hanging his head.

"Evan, the wall does not show what happens after you face Aegir," Lazonia said calmly. "You must fulfill your destiny. You must and will stop Aegir. I believe in you."

"So do I," chimed Claire. "Now, let's go kick some sea-god booty!"

Although Evan was terrified, he laughed at his sister's comment. "I don't see you guys carved on the wall. I thought all of us were going to stick together. I never imagined I would have to face Aegir alone," Evan said and then looked at Lazonia. "Where is everyone else?"

Wearing a frown on her face, the mermaid shook her head. "For whatever reason, you are meant to battle Aegir alone."

Evan sighed and looked at each one of his friends'

117

faces in turn. Dunkle looked most concerned, and he was the one to approach Evan.

"We will travel with you as far as we are permitted. You can do this," said the imp. And although it was impossible to smell anything underwater, Evan believed the area around him was saturated by the odor of pine.

"Perhaps, it is time to see my father," said Lazonia. "I will not be able to swim all of you there. So, I promise to move slowly."

On the journey back, Lazonia stayed true to her word and moved along with the group. Occasionally, she would swim away long enough to speak with a sea turtle or fish, but she always returned.

Half an hour passed before they reached some outer buildings, all of which were made of colorful glass. Etchings and molded sculptures depicted sea life: shells, fish, merpeople, and other ornate designs.

"We need to swim to the top of this building," said Lazonia, coming to a stop. "It is pretty high. Would any of you like for me to help you swim?"

Evan was just about to say yes when Claire snipped, "We'll be fine." And Evan had to scale the building on his own.

CHAPTER EIGHTEEN

TRAVEL BY TURTLE

B Y THE TIME EVAN REACHED the top, Lazonia was already inside the building. Evan drifted into the room, and saw she was already speaking with her father. Evan paused in the center of the circle and was all too aware of the thirteen sets of eyes fixed on him.

"Ah, Sigurd, it is good to see you, old friend," announced Ragnar. "Please, all of you come in."

Sigurd led the group right across and over the circle's center, coming to rest on Ragnar's right side. The two discussed something so quietly that Evan was unable to make out what they were saying. Sigurd then nodded and returned to Claire, Dunkle, and Barfel.

Ragnar began formally, "My fellow council members, we are joined by Evan's sister Claire, Dunkle, Barfel, and—I am certain you all have heard of the great hero—Sigurd."

A flurry of comments were made, but all in undertones. Evan looked around, trying to figure out what was being said. It was no use. Most of the council members were speaking in that funny clicking-fishy language.

And then, for some strange reason, Dunkle gasped.

119

Evan turned to see what had startled the imp but saw nothing unusual other than that a fish arrived and had positioned itself between Lazonia and Ragnar.

"That's him! That's him!" cried out Barfel, pointing his gangly arm at the fish.

Evan had absolutely no clue why the imps were so worked up. It was just a fish. Wait a minute; that fish looked awfully familiar. It was at that moment something occurred to Evan. "Hey, it's the fish from the boat! He's one of Aegir's spies. We caught him with a fishing pole." There were gasps of horror, and Evan flinched. "Okay, not good. Look, we put him in a tub of water and kept him on board. He admitted to being a spy!"

Ragnar leaned over and listened to something the fish had to say. The merman smiled and nodded his head.

"What did the fish say? And how did it get here? We left it on that boat," said Evan, causing even more hostility amongst the mercouncil. "Look, we didn't mistreat it. Obviously its fine," he added, trying to calm the angry merfolk.

"Council members, this boy did not cause the fish, Egbert, any harm," announced Ragnar. "Evan speaks the truth; Egbert is one of Aegir's spies. He has confided in me some of Aegir's plans. We must listen to what he has to say."

"Why should we trust it?" Evan asked, giving the fish a dirty look. "I mean, isn't it one of the bad guys?"

"My dear boy," said Ragnar, "Aegir is neither a 'bad guy' nor is he our enemy. Aegir's outlook of the world has been skewed, warped. He believes that by wiping out mankind, he will be washing away all of his evils."

"Doesn't Aegir realize he'll be washing away all the good stuff too?" said Evan.

"I think that over the centuries, Aegir has forgotten," said Ragnar. "Egbert told me that many sea creatures have forgotten men still have a few virtuous qualities.

In fact, ironically enough, it was not the act of a man that changed the mind of this fish. It was the act of an imp that caused Egbert to reconsider his loyalty. For although Egbert cares little for mankind, he is rather fond of imps and does not wish to see them drowned." Ragnar grinned at Barfel, and Barfel beamed in return.

Barfel leapt into the center of the room and danced around Evan. "Barfel set him free! Barfel set him free!"

Dunkle approached the dancing imp, rested his hand on Barfel's shoulder, and said, "I did not see you release the fish. How were you able to manage it without my knowledge?"

"More importantly, *why* did you?" mumbled Evan, receiving many furious glares. He shrunk back, and grunted, "Sorry."

"Last one off the ship! Dumped him back in the sea!" sang Barfel.

"Good job," said Dunkle, escorting Barfel back to Sigurd and Claire.

"In that one single act, the imp was able to change Egbert's mind about flooding the planet," explained Ragnar, and more discussion ensued. "Now, it's time to tell you everything I know."

Words poured out from the merman's mouth, filling every space. Ragnar wove a tale, sounding more like fiction than fact. Unfortunately for Evan, he happened to play a huge role in the story. "Evan and his comrades must continue traveling to Hlesey. That is where they will find Aegir and the Serpent's Ring. This boy is mankind's only hope for salvation. Although he keeps company with four other heroes, in the end, it will be Evan Jones who must face Aegir—alone," announced Ragnar. "We merpeople will help in any way we can."

"But why?" Claire asked. "I mean, why would you help mankind?"

"We might be creatures of the sea, but we are also

half-human. We believe in the ingenuity of mankind. It will take time, but the oceans will one day return to their former perfection: pure and unspoiled. In his fury, Aegir has lost his way. Although some creatures of the sea agree with him, many do not. Ran's Undersea Hall sits empty. The sea god and goddess have drawn a line so deep in the sand that few have crossed over to their side. Thus, they are alienated from the remainder of Sagaas."

Evan edged back toward the balcony, and just when he was about to make a "swim" for it, Ragnar said, "The hour is late, and you need to rebuild your strength. You will stay here tonight, so as morning breaks you will be ready to complete your task."

"Sir, I have one question for you; if you don't mind," said Claire. "Our submarines are made from wood and are now sitting in a broken heap. We will need materials to make a new submarine."

"What sort of materials do you require?" he asked.

"Metal would be best. That is if you know where I could find some," said Claire.

Ragnar pondered, his fingertips resting together. "Lazonia, please take them to the undersea grotto, and then show them to their quarters."

"Yes, Father," she said dutifully and kissed him fondly on the cheek. In a flash, she was next to Evan, reaching for his hand. "Come with me."

She led them to the balcony and sang something that sounded like, "whaahhh-oooh."

Evan started to ask what she was doing but was quieted by Sigurd. "You must not interrupt her. She is soliciting help."

"Look, over there," said Claire softly.

At first, it looked like five green eggs were bobbing along in the water. After a minute, Evan realized the eggs were actually giant sea turtles, heading in their direction.

"Since you do not swim very fast, I thought it would be easier to travel by turtle," said Lazonia, as the turtles reached the balcony.

"Is that what you were doing? Calling sea turtles to give us a lift?" Evan asked.

"Duh, Evan," said Claire, moving closer to the turtles.

"THEY ARE HUGE," said Evan.

"We will travel quickly. Make sure you hold on tight," instructed Lazonia, and then one of the turtles moaned something from deep in his throat. Lazonia nodded and ran her hand along the back of his neck. "Oh, but please do not squeeze them too tight. And no digging in your heels or tugging on their shells. Remember, they are not seahorses."

Once everyone was situated on his or her sea turtle, Lazonia gave a command, and the turtles raced forward. The turtles and their passengers sped past buildings, heading in the direction of a large cluster of coral reef. As they approached, an opening in the reef came into view.

The sea turtles slowed to a crawl and then allowed their riders to climb off. Lazonia said something and away they went.

"The turtles will come back for us if we need them," she said and swam toward the cave.

Darkness covered the group like a thick blanket. Evan could barely see his hand in front of him, when all of a sudden gems from Lazonia's tail began to glow. Evan's racing heart slowed, and he followed her deep into the heart of the cave.

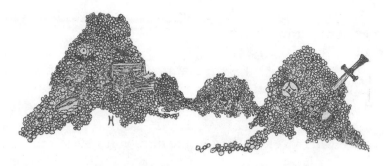

CHAPTER NINETEEN

DRIPPING IN DIAMONDS

AT FIRST, THE CAVE'S WALLS were stark and foreboding, but as Lazonia moved along, resident flora and fauna emerged from holes and deep pits. Evan was so distracted by the spectacle that he accidently bumped right into Claire.

"Oops, sorry," he said, feeling mildly embarrassed. "I couldn't help it. The walls are coming to life."

"Just try to watch where you're going."

Staying focused was virtually impossible for Evan, he was far too entertained. In fact, he repeatedly turned his head to watch the long tunnel become even more vibrant and bright. It reminded him of a fireworks show, only better.

At last, the tunnel opened into an underwater cavern. Lazonia floated over a smooth rock and closed her eyes. She chanted some words, which Evan had never before heard. Water gurgled and then rumbled. It spun around the group, creating a whirlpool. And then, just like a gigantic sink, jelly water drained down through holes in the floor.

The bubble covering Evan's face deflated. He was breathing actual air.

"Come with me and stay close. Otherwise, you will get lost," said Lazonia.

Flickering light shimmered from every crevice, giving the illusion of warmth. For the first time since entering the cavern, Evan looked at Lazonia. Her tail had transformed—she had legs! Gems now wrapped over her like a bodysuit. Other than having purple color on her toenails, her feet and ankles were bare. Gems created swirling patterns around her body. Evan might not have had a whole lot of fashion sense, but he knew this outfit was cool.

Claire rushed toward Lazonia, exclaiming, "Wow, you look stunning. I love how the amethysts and sapphires mix together and sparkle. I want an outfit like yours."

Evan could practically see the wheels spin in Claire's head.

"You can do that later," said Evan, trying to nudge her along.

"Right," she said and followed Lazonia.

Lazonia ventured in the direction of a playful dolphin carved around an enormous, round hole. She wandered through its center and into another dark tunnel, but as Lazonia passed through, the walls sprang to life. Evan took a minute to study the many different phosphorescent shapes. Some were long and cylindrical, with blue and green lines. Others were round with numerous miniscule spheres attached to its surfaces.

"Evan, hurry up! You won't believe this!" Claire shouted from several yards away.

He realized he was far behind and raced to catch up. Sigurd and Claire could be seen beyond a cavernous threshold. Their wide eyes sparkled and twinkled.

"What is it? What do you see?" Evan asked, but they didn't answer.

He ran faster and practically knocked into them with his speed. He looked around, and what he saw made his mouth drop. Mounds of colorful gems, elaborate swords, marble statues, decorative vases, filigreed platters, oversize goblets, and lots and lots of golden coins filled the grotto.

"What is this place?" Claire asked.

"The Grotto," answered Sigurd. I've heard of it, but not in my wildest dreams believed it was real."

"It is very real. We have collected rare treasures for thousands of years. Some were gifts, but many were found in the ships Aegir sank," she said.

"Aegir sinks ships, on purpose?" Evan asked.

"Sometimes," said Lazonia, shrugging her shoulders.

"Why did you bring us here?" Claire asked.

"My father has offered to let you use what you need. It is important for you to succeed on your quest," answered Lazonia.

"I don't suppose that means I could design my own bodysuit with gems?" Claire asked. "I mean, I've been wearing the same clothes for days. I just know I could be more successful if I didn't feel like a drowned rat."

Lazonia smiled and said, "I believe you are right in that. I am certain Father would not mind. After all, you are equally as important on this quest."

The imps played on hills of gold coins, sliding down slopes and then scurrying back up again. Claire giggled, as she dug through piles and piles of perfect gems.

"Ooh, rubies and emeralds! I think I'll make my suit red and green," she announced.

"Great, then you'll look like a Christmas decoration," laughed Evan.

"Good point," she said and dug some more.

"I will search for some proper shields and swords," said Sigurd, wandering over to a far wall lined with golden armory.

Evan looked over at Lazonia. "Thanks," he said simply.

"For what?" she asked.

"You know, helping us."

"Evan, merpeople understand how important it is you retrieve the Serpent's Ring. You have our support."

"Yeah, I know. But I haven't seen any other merpeople helping us the way you have."

"Maybe *this* merperson supports you a little more than the others," she said with a sweet smile.

"Hey guys! I did it! Look over here!" announced Claire.

It was difficult to draw his attention away from Lazonia, but he finally looked over at his sister. She was poised on top of a mountain of golden coins, wearing a ridiculous smirk. She spun around a few times all the while wiggling her hips.

"So, what do you think?" she asked, still prancing around in circles.

"About what?" Evan asked, not really caring.

"You are dazzling," said Sigurd. As if in a trance, he moved over to Claire and appeared appropriately awestruck. Claire rushed to him and smiled brightly.

"You think so?" she asked.

Evan didn't pay attention to what Sigurd said in return. Quite honestly, Evan didn't really care. But he did take a closer look at his sister's new outfit. Starting as a simple strap around one shoulder, diamonds and sapphires trailed down to her knees. It was pretty nice, but didn't hold a candle to Lazonia's. And Evan smiled at the mermaid once more.

"Time to make a sub! Time to make a sub!" announced Barfel, bounding up and down in the middle of the group.

After a few more seconds of mushy-gushy talk between Claire and Sigurd, and the imp finally had everyone's attention.

"What should I build?" Claire asked.

"Aren't you going to make another shark-pod?" Evan asked excitedly. After all, he wanted to travel to Hlesey disguised as a shark. How cool would that be?

"We need to make something bigger, so we can travel in it together," said Sigurd. "Besides, we will have to take turns paddling the blades."

"Paddling? But you didn't have to paddle the shark-pods. Why can't you make a larger sub like that?" Evan asked.

"The wood from Sigurd's ship held energy from the gods, remember?" said Claire. "We were able to make it move by magic. Even if I knew how to make a motor, it wouldn't work. I don't have gasoline; I don't know how to create electricity; and I doubt we could find enough seahorse power to get us where we need to go. Sigurd's right, we'll have to make a stationary bike inside or something to help turn the propellers."

"Well, that stinks," said Evan, shoving his hands into his pockets.

"I think I know what to make," Claire said and wandered over to some gold.

She circled around and around a humongous pile of coins. Then, she paused and threw out her arms. The mound rattled and coins flew into the air. A thousand golden objects hovered for a moment before slamming together. A loud *BOOM* echoed, hurting Evan's ears. Each coin melted together, molding into the shape of a humpback whale. Sea glass melted and molded into dome-shaped observation windows. More circular windows lined the body. On the tips of each fin were golden paddles, and at the tail was a rudder. Evan could only imagine what it looked like inside.

"Wow," he said and rushed to peek through one of the windows.

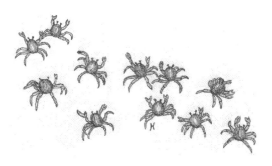

CHAPTER TWENTY

TWIRLING AND FLIPPING

EVAN USED HIS POWERS TO lift the whale-pod. It hovered for a bit, and then traveled out of the grotto, down the tunnel, and back to the open undersea cavern. Once the whale-pod was submerged in water, Evan rushed over. He found an open latch and climbed inside. Lazonia was right on his heels, followed by the imps, and then Sigurd and Claire. The whale-pod was big enough to hold the entire group.

At the front, the whale's mouth formed a massive window-bubble. It served as the operation deck. Below the thick glass were old-fashioned steering wheels and levers; two golden swivel chairs were attached to the floor; and in the center of the pod sat two stationary bicycles with long chains attached to both fins. Evan had a sinking feeling he would soon have to pedal a bike.

"How are we going to breathe once we're underwater?" Claire asked. "I don't know how to make oxygen."

"Leave that to me," chimed Lazonia. "All I have to do is seal all the windows with a similar casing to our bubbles. It will work the same way, bringing oxygen in and carbon dioxide out." Lazonia hurried around the sub, sealing off each window.

Thankfully, the imps seemed delighted at being able to ride stationary bikes. And since Sigurd was busy organizing his newly acquired collection of shields and swords, Evan was left to steer. He raced to the front and sat in the captain's chair. Claire instructed him on how to operate the levers and knobs and wheels.

"Are you ready to see what this machine can do?" Evan asked as he began to take command of the whale-pod.

Evan submerged the vessel under the water and started traveling back down the long tunnel. Unfortunately, Sigurd returned sooner than expected and sat next to Evan. To Evan's surprise, Sigurd didn't try to take over. Instead, he simply helped navigate through the dark tunnel.

The whale-pod maneuvered rather well, considering its massive size and rudimentary construction. It didn't take long to return to what Evan now referred to as Mertopia. Lazonia directed Evan on where to park, leaning ever so slightly over his shoulder. A strand of her violet hair brushed his face, and he could swear he smelled lavender—a pleasing scent.

The group exited through a primitive diving hatch. Instantly, like dropping water on a sponge, Lazonia's tail returned. She briskly recreated bubbles on everyone's faces and throats.

Lazonia rushed over to a towering yellow building and entered through the swiveling doors. Once inside, she approached another mermaid. They spoke for a minute before Lazonia returned to the group.

"Good news—the council has arranged for each of you to stay in your own suite," she said excitedly.

"Oh, I hope there are actual beds. I'd love to have a good night's rest," sighed Claire.

"The beds might be slightly different from what you are used to, but I believe you will sleep well," said Lazonia. "I will accompany you to your rooms. We can meet back here in an hour, and I will take you to dinner."

The group was led by another mermaid through a lobby of sorts. Evan looked up and was reminded of a nautilus shell. There wasn't a ceiling, and Evan could see all the way up and through the building. A sloped balcony wound its way along the walls, swirling up higher and higher.

Below the lobby floor was an aquarium, but instead of holding water, it was sandy and dry. Air was sealed inside the pocket where crabs scurried around and burrowed holes.

Lazonia and the other mermaid swam up the balcony, round and round. As soon as they reached the top, they paused. Dunkle and Barfel were each led into their rooms, as were Claire and Sigurd. Finally, Evan reached his suite. The door had rounded corners, a slightly bulged out center, and a starfish design etched into its surface.

"I will wait for you in the lobby. See you in an hour," Lazonia said and before swimming away added, "After you shut the door, press the round button."

"Okay, thanks," said Evan, entering his room.

Lazonia was right; this room was nothing like he was accustomed to. Evan shut the door and looked for the button. It wasn't difficult to find being that it was at least the size of a baseball. He hesitated for a second before pressing it. What was going to happen? He shrugged his shoulders and pushed it. Suddenly, he heard a clunking sound and tiny holes opened beneath him. In one instantaneous movement, water disappeared, draining through the floor. The room was filled with oxygen and Evan's face-bubble collapsed. He inhaled the salty air, held it in his lungs, and then let it out.

Everything in the room was translucent yellow and orange with veins of pulsating colors laced throughout: the egglike chair, the turtle sculpture, and even the bathroom in the corner. He stared at the seahorse-shaped tub and shower, but why would he bathe after having been in water for an entire day?

"Where's the bed?" he wondered out loud.

Across the room was a large dome-shaped window. It too was yellow, but unlike the walls, he could see through it perfectly. As he wandered over to check out the view, he felt something squishy under his feet. He looked down and discovered he was standing on a bed. It was level with the floor and although it was difficult to see its edges, he was relatively certain it was circular in shape. He went to his knees and felt the mushy surface. It was like being on a waterbed, except its center was filled with some sort of foam. Each time he pressed down and lifted his hand, his impression remained into its surface. Evan knew he'd sleep well.

An hour passed, and Evan was ready to rejoin his group. When he tried to open the door, he discovered it wouldn't budge. He nudged and pushed, trying not to panic. Finally, he remembered the round button. He pressed it, the room refilled with water, and the door slid opened. A bubble appeared out of a hole next to the door and stretched over his face.

Down in the lobby, Dunkle and Barfel crawled around, tapping on the floor-aquarium. Crabs followed their movements, twirling and flipping along with the imps.

"Are you ready to eat?" Lazonia asked.

"Yes, I'm starving," said Claire.

Lazonia led them to a tube-shaped hallway. They walked inside, and it lit up yellow. The color slowly melded with orange and then purple. By the time they reached the restaurant, the entire room was blue. The design inside was simple, but when put with ever-changing wall colors, it was mesmerizing.

A fish waiter greeted them and led them to a circular booth. Of course, Claire rushed to sit beside Sigurd. They were then sandwiched between the two imps. Evan and Lazonia were forced to sit on either end. Lazonia ordered food with her clicks and clacks, and Evan watched his sister's reaction with glee. He realized that only a few hours ago, he had worn that same look of confusion.

In minutes, six individual meals, enclosed by bubbles, came to their table. Instead of sticks of seaweed frisatta, there were round nuggets. Evan wasn't sure what they were, but one thing was certain, they weren't fish.

Claire poked at the bubble with the tip of her finger a few times and inquired, "How are we supposed to eat this?"

"Don't you know anything?" Evan said sarcastically. "Watch and learn from the master."

Effortlessly, he dipped in his hand and retrieved a white nugget. He tossed it up and then caught it in his mouth.

"What is it? Some sort of fish?" Claire asked, still poking at her plate.

Lazonia's eyes constricted, and Evan jumped in. "Claire, how could you even suggest these merpeople would eat fish? I mean really, do you actually think they're cannibals or something?" Evan said smugly and leaned back against his seat, trying to conceal a faint smirk. Yeah, he enjoyed embarrassing his sister.

"By the way, what is this?" Evan whispered to Lazonia.

"It is a salad made with shoo-shoo and seaweed," she said.

"Well, I don't know what shoo-shoo is, but it's good," Evan said and continued to enjoy his dinner.

"Shoo-shoo is a little like your tofu," said Lazonia.

"I've never been a fan of tofu, but this shoo-shoo is

good," said Evan, eating another piece. "Where do you find all of your food? Do you have a farm on land or something?"

"No, silly. We have an underwater greenhouse," said Lazonia, waving a piece of shoo-shoo around as she spoke. "Mostly, we use hydroponics. Where do you think land dwellers learned how to cultivate plants without using soil?"

"I don't know. I never really thought about it," said Evan.

At which Claire added, "Or cared."

"Claire, I care about hydroponics," interjected Evan. "In fact, I want to grow tomatoes. Wasn't I saying, just the other day, how great it would be if we had fresh tomatoes?"

Claire laughed, "Whatever, Evan."

"She doesn't know what she's talking about," Evan said to Lazonia. Feeling his face burn red, he tried to casually eat a strand of seaweed.

That night, Evan fell into a restless sleep. Dreams came to him again, and he found himself standing on the edge of a rocky cliff. The waves grew bigger and bigger, crashing just below his bare feet. Sharp rocks cut into his soles. He ignored the pain and focused instead on the giant waves.

Colorful bull sharks swam, and a stingray, the size of a small plane, emerged from the deep blue. Various shades of yellow and green spun together, creating an intricate design along the stingray's wings. Sharks circled in slow and calculated movements, while the stingray swished between, moving rapidly. Sea creatures merged together, forming militarylike ranks, as if gearing up for battle. Evan reached his hands back and ran them along the cliff's jagged surface. He looked down the rocky mountain, wondering how he ended up there.

After lifting his head, he stared at the wall of sharks and stingrays. He would have to fight. All of his energy went into the center of the wave, creating a spiraling vortex. Sharks and stingrays swirled around the whirlpool. Evan intensified his stare. Back, back, back … he focused and pushed. To his surprise, the sea did as he commanded, edging away in defeat.

"That's it!" shouted Evan. "I can do this!"

With all of his strength, he drove back the giant wave, and the smaller ones followed. The wind disappeared. Slowly, Evan opened his eyes. He was no longer on the cliff. He was safe on his orange, squishy waterbed—at least for the moment.

The next morning, after an interesting breakfast, it was time to start their journey. Lazonia escorted them to the whale-pod. Claire swam next to her, gloating about the good night's sleep she had. According to her, the bed was amazing, and the shower was heaven. Evan realized he hadn't bothered with the shower, now he wished he had.

They entered the whale-pod through a diving hatch at the bottom. As soon as they were in the dry compartment, Lazonia's tail returned to legs covered with amethysts and sapphires.

"That is so cool," Claire said and followed Sigurd to the front.

"I guess this is goodbye," said Evan, reaching for Lazonia's hand. "Thanks for everything."

"What do you mean goodbye? I am coming with you," she said flatly.

"No, you aren't."

"Yes, I am," Lazonia fired back.

"Your father never said you could come with us. It's too dangerous. I can't let you."

"Unfortunately, you have no choice. I am coming," she said in a tone that not only matched Evan's, it was far sterner. "I have a feeling you will need me."

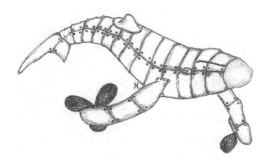

CHAPTER TWENTY-ONE

GOLDEN WHALE-POD

Dunkle and Barfel took to their bikes, peddling vigorously and leaving Evan and Claire to man the front. After Lazonia instructed them on which way to start, she and Sigurd went to the next room to discuss their direction and strategy. For the first time since leaving Terra, Claire and Evan were alone.

"So, what do you think Mom and Dad are doing? Do you think they're worried?" Evan whispered.

"Panicked is more like it. Do you remember the time you went to the bathroom at that water park and didn't tell anyone? Mom had the entire lifeguard staff searching the pools for you," Claire said with a slight laugh.

"Yeah. That was really embarrassing. Funny thing is that I miss them. I wish we could see them."

"Maybe we can," said Claire, pulling out her locket. "We want to see Mom and Dad."

Colors changed into fog. The view traveled through clouds and back to Greenfield Village. There, in the center, was the clock tower. The time read 11:59. The scene showed Evan's parents, sitting on a bench. His dad anxiously tapped his foot and continued to look at his watch. His voice was muffled, but Evan could make out that he was asking Mom where Claire and Evan could be.

Mom looked equally concerned but told him not to worry. Finally, Dad's foot stopped tapping. The image pulled back and scanned the clock. It read 12:00. Abruptly, the oval mirror returned to a mixture of colors, and then back to a steely gray mirror.

"That was when we were supposed to meet them," snapped Evan. "What happened next?"

Claire continued to ask questions about their parents, but nothing further was revealed.

"That's it; that's all we're going to see," rationalized Claire.

Dunkle and Barfel cheered as they pedaled their bikes. Not that Evan was lazy or anything, but he didn't want to ride on a stationary bike if he didn't have to.

⁓⚬⚭⚬•

They had traveled for a few hours when Lazonia returned. She pointed toward the empty sea and said, "Pretty soon, there will be a large rock formation, shaped like the profile of an old man."

"What are we going to do next? I mean, did you and Sigurd come up with a plan?" Evan asked.

"We decided we should travel underneath the island, to an opening in the rock formation. It is not used very often, and I believe we will be able to arrive, unnoticed," explained Lazonia.

"What about once we are in there? What do we do then?" Evan asked anxiously.

"We have not figured that part out yet," said Lazonia. "Evan, please do not look so worried; we will come up with a plan."

"Right, even if it develops as we go," added Sigurd, after entering the chamber.

138

"Great," said Evan, slouching down in his seat.

"Look, there it is," exclaimed Lazonia.

Dunkle and Barfel's little legs moved so speedily they became a blur. The whale-pod tore through water, straight for the "Rock of Terror." At least, that was what Evan now called it.

"I can see an opening over there," Claire announced excitedly.

"There's no rush. Really guys, it's not like we have to wear ourselves out trying to get there," said Evan, but everyone just stared at him.

They entered a foreboding tunnel, and Evan wasn't certain, but he thought he saw a few human skeletons here and there. Of course, he could have been imagining things. But the farther and deeper they traveled, the more Evan's stomach twisted and turned. He wondered how he could get out of this mess. He tried to remember what Lazonia had said about Aegir not being such a bad guy. But what if she was wrong?

The water had an eerie glow, and up ahead, it fizzed and popped and gurgled. Unfortunately, they were heading right in that direction. It didn't take long for the entire whale-pod to become engulfed by fluorescent-green water.

"We need to go up to where the cavern opens," directed Lazonia.

Evan's heart pounded in his chest, beating in his ears. His head felt light, as if it were becoming detached from his body. Gradually, everything went dark. Evan struck something and pain radiated all the way down to his toes. He could feel someone shake him.

"Evan, Evan, are you alright?" Claire's voice cut through the darkness.

A pinpoint of light appeared far away, and then slowly enlarged to include the entire room. Evan had to shield his eyes. He sat up and realized he had been lying flat on the gilded floor. He was still in the submarine.

"Are you all right? You just fell over," said Lazonia, trying to help him stand.

"I'm not sure," strained Evan.

"Yuck! You're all clammy," said Claire, wiping her hands off on his T-shirt.

"Hey, I've been under some pressure here!" blurted Evan defensively.

"Sorry. You must be scared to death," sympathized Claire.

"Well, I'm not exactly looking forward to taking the Serpent's Ring back from Aegir," said Evan.

"You're going to have to pull it together. You can't pass out when you are face to face with Aegir," reminded Claire.

They emerged up inside a square, metal room, lit only by a greenish glow. Sigurd maneuvered the whale-pod beside an embankment and stared out through the glass bubble. It looked like they had entered a bank vault, with perfectly lined corners.

"Are you ready?" Lazonia asked.

Evan nodded, and with feigned confidence, walked up the circular staircase. While holding his breath, he lifted the hatch. He climbed down the outside of the wet whale-pod carefully and landed on a smooth stone platform. The ground was slick, and he slipped. He fell back and let out his reserve of air. Immediately, he felt a rush of spearmint enter his mouth. Mist came off the water and clung to his skin, making him shiver. His lips now tingled and tasted like mouthwash. His eyes burned and watered up.

"Lazonia, I breathed in this minty air!" yelled Evan, as Lazonia climbed down to the platform.

"You need to get out of there," said Lazonia. "Hurry over to that center door and pull down the lever. There will be a hallway on the other side. The effervescence will not be as strong in there."

Evan stood and pulled down the eel-shaped lever, and the door shot up. It was dark on the other side, and Evan hesitated before rushing through. Light began to sizzle above his head. Eels! They lined the ceiling, lighting his way. Evan was certain he saw one of them move, but surely they couldn't have still been alive. He scanned the length of the hall; its entire length was plated in steel. He studied the metal bolts that lined the seams. Each one was in the shape of a different shell.

After the entire group was close enough, he asked, "Now what?"

"Now, we travel to the Undersea Hall. It won't be very far," said Lazonia. "I will go first."

"I shall go first," said Sigurd, easing his way forward. "If we are attacked, I will be able to fight whatever it is. At least that might give you some time to reach Aegir."

"Sigurd, nobody's here," said Evan. "I'm sure we'll slip in unnoticed."

"One can never be certain about anything," said Sigurd, now leading the group.

Claire sighed and followed her hero. Evan was stuck back near the imps, who reeked of fear. Worse yet, the space was cramped, making it difficult to endure the odor of frightened imp.

At last, they reached the Undersea Hall's entrance. Evan sighed in relief. Just as he had hoped, it was deserted—eerie, but deserted.

The walls next to Evan were rocky at first, but as he continued to walk, its surface changed. Crushed shells, with a pearlescent sheen, decorated the walls, continuing all the way up to the ridiculously high ceiling.

"See, I told you, we'll be able to sneak in. No one will know we're here," said Evan.

"I do not think we will be so lucky," said Sigurd, pointing toward a wall. "Look over there."

Forms, in the shape of men, protruded out from the wall. Each of their faces resembled crumbling stone busts in a graveyard.

"What's the big deal?" Evan asked, still staring at the figures' vacant expressions.

"I am not entirely certain; however, I have an ominous feeling," said Sigurd.

Wisps of smoke came from the ground, spiraling and spinning. The vapor separated, streaming toward each individualized form. Life sparked inside the human shapes, and they began to move. Each of their bodies stretched out from the wall. Slowly, their vague features defined. Crushed shells pressed deeper into their bodies and deepened in color. Some were death black and others were corpse pale. Now, fully formed, they dragged their heavy bodies to the center of the floor.

The twelve guards remained motionless, strategically positioned like pawns on a chessboard. Each was equal in size and shape but held a different piece of battle armor in their colossal hands: swords, axes, clubs with spikes, clubs without spikes, and spears. Even more intimidating were the few without weapons.

CHAPTER TWENTY-TWO

FEISTY DRAUGAR

"WHAT ARE THEY?" CLAIRE ASKED, hiding behind Sigurd. "Are they guards?"

"They are something like that. They are the draugar," said Sigurd. He stared ahead, his body tensing.

"Sigurd, even you are not strong enough to battle twelve draugar," said Lazonia. "We must go back."

"Sigurd, where did they come from?" Evan asked.

"They were once sailors on the great seas," answered Sigurd. "That was before Ran captured them in her golden net, one by one."

"She does not mean to kill them!" interjected Lazonia. "Once a sailor promises to worship her ... well, let's just say she quickly realizes how fragile humans are."

"Yes, time and time again," scoffed Sigurd. "In the end, she always wins. They forever serve her, guarding both her Undersea Hall and all of her treasures."

"There are only twelve of them," said Evan. "I watched Sigurd and Claire battle against more giants than that."

"Evan," said Lazonia, shaking her head. "Not only does a draugr possess superhuman strength, they can change into other creatures. Plus, they are already dead.

Only a hero can defeat them, and it is extremely difficult."

"But, Sigurd is a hero," said Evan.

"But, there are twelve of them," said Claire.

Finally, Sigurd addressed the guards. "Allow us to pass. We seek council with Aegir and Ran."

The draugar did not budge or react at all to Sigurd's request.

"They're not moving. Maybe we should try to go around them," said Evan. "I'll go first."

Evan had already begun to skirt around the draugar, when Sigurd shouted, "Evan, no!!"

Just then, Evan heard something shuffle. He peered over at the draugar. They hadn't budged, but strangely their bodies were contorting; their chests heaved and their shoulders widened. The guard closest to Evan cricked his neck—*creech!*—and stared right at Evan.

"Ah!" cried out Evan.

"Evan, get out of there!" shouted Claire.

Evan ran and screamed and did not look back until something smashed down to the ground. The sound ricocheted, and Evan turned around.

Lazonia hollered after him, "Keep going Evan! We will be okay! They are leaving us alone and only following you!"

Evan had almost reached a short flight of steps, when a catlike creature pounced on top of him. It was small, the size of an alley cat, but extremely heavy. It too was ghoulish. Its yellow eyes closed in on Evan. Soon, they were nose to nose.

"Get off me!" yelled Evan, swatting at the creepy cat.

Evan struggled, but could not get the cat off his chest. Although it didn't move, Evan could feel its weight begin to increase. It wasn't getting bigger, just heavier. The pressure on Evan's ribcage was unbearable. Pretty soon, his bones were going to snap. When, suddenly, the blade from Sigurd's sword flashed above, and the cat's head was dislodged from its body.

"Sigurd, look behind you!" yelled Claire. She, Lazonia, and the imps had remained behind. It seemed the draugar didn't show any interest in those who did not try to cross their path. But now, Evan and Sigurd were in serious trouble.

"Evan, you must go into the Undersea Hall and find Aegir," instructed Sigurd.

"What about you?"

"Do not worry about me. Go—NOW!" said Sigurd as he spun around and slashed his sword into the chest of another draugr.

Evan darted up a flight of steps. Just a few feet more and he would reach the entrance to the Undersea Hall. A warm and inviting glow came from the other side of the gigantic entryway. The entire wall was made up of wooden archways and beams. The beams created a honeycomb pattern, stretching up four stories high.

Clank! Crash! Evan turned to see what had happened. Sigurd continued to battle against one of the draugr. The other nine guards held tight to their positions and hadn't moved, staring straight ahead at Evan's friends. Sigurd was the only one in immediate danger. He whipped his blade through the air, chopping off pieces of the draugr, bit by bit—a hand here, a toe there. It was a disgusting sight to behold, but at last, the draugr lay in a broken pile of stones and shells.

Sigurd's hand rested on his knee while he caught his breath. He lifted his head and sweat streamed down his face. He looked over at Evan and hollered, "You need to hurry!"

One of the remaining nine draugar turned around and rushed Sigurd, but Sigurd was too fast and leapt out of the way. Evan couldn't stop watching and had to force himself to back up toward the columns. On both sides of him were large, golden statues. To his right, Aegir and to his left, Ran. Their bodies were angled toward Evan, as if welcoming him.

A sultry voice came from Evan's left, "You are either very foolish or very brave." It was Ran.

"I think I might be a mixture of the two," Evan said without thinking.

Ran laughed, and as she did, the sound reverberated around Evan's head. He winced and covered his ears.

From behind her golden statue she emerged. Her long, wavy hair was held back with seashells. Her eyes were large and blue, and her complexion fair. When she moved, her pale-blue dress shimmered like sunlight dancing over water. And although Evan had been prepared to despise this goddess, in person, he felt a strange fondness for her.

"Your Goddessness, we are here to seek your help," Evan said diplomatically.

"Oh really, Evan Jones, what could you possibly ask of me? You are here to steal away the Serpent's Ring, are you not?" said Ran. "Quite honestly, I am surprised you are bold enough to approach me."

"Please, I need to speak with you and Aegir," said Evan.

"I am afraid Aegir is preoccupied at the moment. As you well know, he is unleashing Jormundgand. I, however, am here. So, speak," said Ran.

Evan looked over at Sigurd, who was fighting off yet another draugr. This one swung at Sigurd with an enormous club, knocking the blond hero clear across the floor.

"Your Goddessness, would you be so kind as to call off your guards, at least while we talk?" Evan asked, wincing as Sigurd was being dragged around by his boots.

"I shall, but only if you cease in calling me 'Your Goddessness.' You sound ridiculous," said Ran. "I am

Ran, and would like to be referred to by my name."

"Of course," said Evan.

"My Darling Draugar, you have done well. For now, you may rest," said Ran, and the guards became immobilized.

It was good timing too, since Sigurd's head was about to be squished under a draugr's foot.

"Do you mind if my friends join us?" Evan asked, and Ran nodded.

Claire hurried over to help Sigurd, but Lazonia charged up the steps and stood right in front of Ran.

"It was not always like this," said Lazonia. "There was a time, not long ago, when you shared this hall with merpeople. We were friends and allies for many centuries. It does not have to be like this."

"You are right, my dear little mermaid. Join with us and all will be forgiven," offered Ran.

Lazonia smiled and studied the goddess before speaking, "I have a better plan in mind. You should help us stop Aegir. You must realize his plan is complete nonsense."

"Yeah, and there is still good on land," interjected Evan. "In fact, I still don't understand how oil spilled into the Great Reef. I mean, coral reefs are protected. Ships aren't even allowed to sail near them."

"Are you suggesting my husband and I made up the story of the oil polluting one of our reefs?" fumed Ran.

"No, of course not," said Evan. "It's just that, it doesn't make sense to me how oil spilled there. Sure, oil spills into the oceans all the time, just not on a coral reef."

"I know for a fact, a large ship capsized right in the center of the reef," raged Ran.

Lazonia interrupted, "You must miss having guests fill the Undersea Hall. If Aegir is successful, who will be here to celebrate with you? Help us, and the merpeople will return; land creatures will return; other great gods will return."

"I have heard enough," Ran said and waved her hand.

Water rushed into the open space, pouring in from tunnels and striking the stairs. More and more water filled the room. Waves grew and white crests formed at their peaks.

"Ran, please help us! If Aegir unlocks Jormundgand the entire planet will be flooded!" pleaded Evan.

"You will see; the world will be a better place once it is finished." Ran hung her head and turned to leave. Spearmint-green water gushed up the steps. Sigurd, Claire, and the imps scurried to the top. Evan noticed something strange stir in the water, when faces emerged out of the foaming crests. There were nine of them—all girls.

"It is the daughters of Aegir and Ran," said Lazonia. "We need to run. Not even I can breathe under effervescent water." The group raced through the entrance into the Undersea Hall.

The entire space was prepared for a banquet. Red banners floated in midair. Golden sea creatures swam up and down each piece of rippling fabric. A chill cut through Evan as he looked upon the banner depicting a bull shark. This particular banner just so happened to hang predominantly over the center table. And while all the other wooden tables were rectangular in shape, the one in the center was round and quite a bit larger. From up above, the arrangement would most likely have looked like a starfish or an octopus.

Platters of food covered every table, but nobody feasted. Bubble-shaped aquariums sat upon every table, and inside, deep-sea fish glowed with fluorescent light, but nobody was there to see. Music drifted from a pipe organ made from conch shells. Brown and beige keys moved up and down, but nobody was there to hear its mysterious melody. There were no dancers, but the tentaclelike legs of the tables swayed with the rhythm.

"Ran, remember when Himinglaeva and I danced for you? You have been like a mother to me. Is this what you want? Once you wash away the world, there will be no one to share in your festivities!" Lazonia lashed out, but Ran was nowhere in sight.

Water rushed through, crashing at Evan's feet. Sigurd tried to hurry the group away from the fizzing water, but Lazonia stayed behind. She continued to yell and shout. Oddly, the largest wave halted. A young girl's face came out of the sea foam.

"Himinglaeva, we were friends!" cried Lazonia.

A hush came from the wave, sounding much like a breeze. Water collapsed toward the ground, and a girl appeared.

"Lazonia, we can no longer be friends. It is forbidden," said the girl with long white hair and pearlescent-blue skin.

"Says who? Your father? As far as I am concerned, our fathers' war is not our war," said Lazonia.

"Lazonia—" started Himinglaeva, but she didn't finish, instead, she stood motionless with her eyes looking down.

"Please help us. We need to convince Aegir to change his mind. It is not too late," said Lazonia softly, reaching for her friend's hand.

Ran entered the room. She looked at her daughter and back toward Lazonia. "Lazonia, you must leave this place. No harm will come to you." An expression of wistfulness crossed Ran's face.

"Please, you must listen—" Lazonia started, but was interrupted by Ran.

"I might not completely agree with Aegir, but I will not turn against my husband," she said and rested both hands on Himinglaeva's milky-white shoulders. "Now, leave. Use that door. It will lead you to Aegir. You may try to stop him, but I am afraid you will fail."

Lazonia nodded, but before walking away she tried to plead with her friend. And for the first time, Evan realized Himinglaeva's skin had changed color, rolling from white to various shades of blue. Now, her skin looked a lot like the ocean in a storm. Himinglaeva didn't listen to her friend; instead, she turned her head, burying it in her mother's billowing hair.

"I see," Lazonia said and rejoined the group.

"That was the bravest thing I have ever seen," complimented Claire.

"Brave, maybe, but nothing I said made a difference," said Lazonia, tears streaming down her cheeks.

"We are still alive," said Sigurd. "Obviously, they listened."

The group went quiet for a moment before walking through the Undersea Hall.

"Do you suppose anyone would notice if I took one small piece of food?" said Evan, feeling slightly awkward with his request.

"I am surprised I did not think of that," said Sigurd.

"I am not hungry, but I am certain the food will be delicious. It always was," said Lazonia, wandering past the group and then slouching against a wall.

Evan felt a little awkward picking food off one of Ran's golden plates, but that didn't stop him. There was chicken with a golden crust, mashed potatoes with gravy, a puffed pastry with mushrooms inside, and Norwegian kelp soufflé. Evan reached for a chicken leg and kept walking.

CHAPTER TWENTY-THREE

SNAPPING DOORKNOB

LAZONIA LED THEM TO A small, wooden door. She barely touched its handle when it swung open and slammed into the wall. Evan jumped back upon hearing the loud noise, but still managed to go through the door first. It was dark, very dark. Lazonia screeched and clicked, and a torch on the wall caught fire.

"That was handy," said Evan to Lazonia. He looked in front of him and then up. "Great, we get to climb an old rickety staircase. And look, it goes up into complete darkness."

"I will go first," said Sigurd.

"No, I can do this," said Evan. He had barely placed his bare foot on the first step when the wood cracked.

"I'm not so sure about this," said Evan. "It doesn't look very safe. I really don't want to plummet to my death."

"Maybe this is a trap," said Claire. "I think it's awfully fishy that Ran would help us."

"I know her well, and I know she would not send us into a trap," explained Lazonia. "If she wanted to kill us, she would have done it herself."

"What a nice goddess," Claire said sarcastically and

151

pushed her way to the front of the group. "I'll go first and repair the wood."

She waved her hand over each step before ascending. She continued like this for a while, until finally the staircase ended and led into a tunnel. Ahead, torches sparked to life, and as the group passed, the same vibrant torches simply blinked out.

Occasionally, the tunnel would open into a large cavern and the group would have to cross over wobbly bridges made from old wood and frayed rope. Far below, enormous rock formations protruded up, and although it was difficult to see, Evan could hear water rushing.

The group continued traveling along more stairs and through more tunnels, until finally they reached a carved door. Evan nudged his sister aside and stared at its decoration. There was the image of Jormundgand wrapped around the entire planet.

"This is it," whispered Evan, staring at the door. The golden handle was also in the likeness of Jormundgand, but only the serpent's head. Jormundgand's open mouth and pointy teeth were daunting, and Evan debated whether he wanted to touch it.

"Evan, it's only a doorknob," said Claire. "Go on through. We're right behind you."

"All right," he said and reached forward. While the small likeness of Jormundgand was clutched inside Evan's hand it snapped at him! "Argh!" Evan yelled and leapt backward. "The handle tried to bite me!"

"Evan, that's impossible," said Claire.

The eyes on the handle glowed, one red and one blue. It snarled and snapped every time Evan reached for it.

"Great," said Evan. "How are we going to get through?"

"Try your powers," said Claire. "Imagine turning the handle with your mind."

Evan stared at the little monster and tried to open the door using the power of his mind. It didn't work, and the mini Jormundgand growled some more.

"Please, allow me to try," said Dunkle. "The door is immune to your powers. This, however, should do the trick." Dunkle removed his vest. "Evan, as soon as I open the door, you must race through."

"Whatever you say," Evan replied. "But, I seriously doubt you'll be able to open it."

Dunkle swayed from side to side while studying the door handle. Promptly, he tossed his vest over the small serpent and turned the handle. It worked! Evan rushed over and helped push into the heavy door. It barely budged, so Evan rammed into it with his shoulder. He fell through and ended up slipping onto the wet ground on the other side. Claire began to follow, but a tremendous *whoosh* blasted shut the door, right in her face! Evan's friends were stuck on the other side. He jumped up and rushed over. He tugged and pounded and yelled! But it was no use, the door was sealed.

"Evan! Wait for us!" yelled Claire. "Don't do anything stupid!"

Although Evan tried to move the door with telekinesis, he knew it was futile. He hollered, "Dunkle was right, there must be a greater power working here! The door won't budge!"

It was going to be difficult, but Evan knew he was going to face Aegir on his own. And no matter what was to come, it was time to show what he was made of. He turned around and saw that he was standing inside a small cave. Water occupied its center, with only a few feet of ground around the edge.

Evan staggered along until he was finally outside, staring up at the open sky. His choices were grim: jagged rocks behind and turbulent sea in front. The wind was fierce and waves raged below. Ever so carefully, he climbed along a narrow trail that led up and along the mountain's side.

It was difficult, but he finally made it to the other side of the mountain. He wasn't relieved, however; as there, high up in the sky, was the enormous and terrifying face of Jormundgand! Its tail was still clenched in its mouth, but it didn't hold still. No, the tail thrashed around, like a snake caught on fire.

Jormundgand was horrifyingly massive. The serpent's head alone was bigger than the entire University of Michigan football stadium. The giant beast was an appalling sight, with its deep thunderous roar and venom seething like acid from its mouth.

Evan edged his way up the path, getting closer and closer to Jormundgand, until finally, he reached a plateau and couldn't go any farther. This was where he would take his stand. But where was Aegir? Hopefully, the sea god had changed his mind.

The wind beat against Evan, and water rose up the mountain's side. The tide had already covered the cave's door, so it was now underwater. He thought about his sister and friends. How would they find him? Would he ever see them again?

Dark harrowing clouds formed, lightning flashed, and thunder erupted. Rain spilled, making it practically impossible for Evan to stand on the cliff's slippery surface. He clung to grooves along the wall and waited and waited.

Suddenly, Aegir's gargantuan body came up from the sea. His hair was jet black with streaks of turquoise blue. Waves crashed against his barrel chest. White sea foam formed into horses at play, holding their shape for a little while and then dissolving into the waters of the sea.

"You don't have to do this!" Evan shouted and then threw his hand over his mouth.

Aegir shifted his attention away from the Serpent's Ring, focusing it fully onto Evan.

"I must act now. Jormundgand's head moves slowly, taking an entire month to cycle around the world. This is when he visits Hlesey," said the sea god, moving closer to a frightened Evan. "Besides, what does a young boy know of such things?"

"I know your Undersea Hall is empty, except for some food and music. And that your daughter, Himinglaeva, has been isolated from Lazonia. I suspect you have also lost a few allies, along the way," yelled Evan.

"How dare you speak to me about my daughter?" Aegir cried out and moved his hand over the ocean. Now, the sea formed into perfectly structured waves—just like in Evan's nightmares. Several more waves started out as soothing ripples along the ocean's surface. They grew higher and higher, into enormous walls, and then slammed against the rocks.

Evan sank down and cowered. The sea god's boisterous laughter reached down into Evan's core, pushing him into a tighter ball.

"This frightened young boy is what I feared would stop me?" Aegir proclaimed and laughed some more.

Aegir was right, Evan felt foolish. So, he started to inch his way back down the slope. After all, this was crazy; he wouldn't be able to defeat a sea god and serpent.

A wave surged up and crashed against the cliff, blocking Evan. Aegir scowled and lifted his hand higher. A giant wall of water froze a few feet from Evan. Colorful fins from a stingray flashed back and forth, and Evan was being watched by black, round eyes. Bull sharks had come.

The sea god continued to laugh, mocking Evan, when all of a sudden, something was unleashed from deep inside the boy. He became angry. Angry with the taunting and angry with this bully trying to inflict fear! Evan rose to his feet and clenched his fists. He narrowed his eyes and put all of his energy into moving the wave.

It worked! The large sheet of water crept back—the sharks and stingrays swam away. Rain stopped pouring, and the wind came to a halt. Evan wasn't sure if he had caused all of that to happen but was relieved nonetheless.

Aegir stood motionless and watched Evan with apparent interest.

"I may have underestimated you," began Aegir, "except I am afraid it is too late. There is nothing you can do to stop me."

CHAPTER TWENTY-FOUR

FACES IN WAVES

AEGIR TURNED HIS BACK ON Evan and stared up at Jormundgand. Evan hadn't noticed before, but the giant sea serpent was bound by a golden collar. The smooth band had one simple design molded into it. On the area underneath Jormundgand's jaw was an impression of a small, circular ring. Evan couldn't make out the details, but had little doubt it would match the Serpent's Ring.

Slowly, the Serpent's Ring drifted upward. Evan wasn't sure what he could do to stop it, but he had to try something. He pushed himself off the cliff. Water drops slapped his face, stinging his skin and burning his eyes. He jetted around to the back of Aegir and darted for the Serpent's Ring. Lucky for Evan, Aegir was still looking at the collar and had not yet noticed the flying boy.

With lightning speed, Evan caught the Serpent's Ring. He looped around and aimed for the mountain's top. Aegir waved his hand. A wave spat water in Evan's direction with great precision, striking Evan on the back of his head. Everything went black, and he started to spiral down. With all of his might, he tried to focus, but it was useless, and he plummeted toward the raging sea.

157

Just as he was about to crash hard onto the water, something strange happened. Foam bubbled up and cushioned Evan's fall.

"Take this, Evan. Give it to Aegir," whispered the water, and it spouted up like a geyser, propelling Evan higher and higher and closer and closer to Aegir. Something small and round was clenched inside Evan's fist. What could it be? He opened his hand ... Claire's locket! Evan didn't have time to open it, and there was no time to consider his options. Aegir's large hand swatted, barely missing Evan. The geyser lifted Evan to just above Aegir's open palm and froze. Evan didn't think; he tossed the locket into the sea god's hand and yelled, "You need to look at this!" And with that, the waterspout turned away and headed back toward the rocky cliff.

A column of white foam cradled Evan, as it raced over the sea; that was, until he was tossed through the air. Luckily, he landed safely on his hands and knees. He lifted his head and looked for the sea foam; it was now returning to Aegir.

"Father, you must look inside the locket," whispered the wave.

Aegir's face reddened, and he howled, "What is the meaning of this?"

A girl's face formed along the crest, and her finger rested on her lips. "Shhhh. Father, open the locket. It will show you what you need to see."

Claire's locket began to glow. It opened up, and sparks of color reflected off Aegir's stricken face. He looked down and watched as the reflective surface revealed a message. Aegir's skin paled, and his thunderous voice echoed, "Dufa!"

Evan was incredibly confused until he was approached by the sea goddess herself. "I am impressed by your bravery, young man," Ran's cool voice came from behind. "You are an exception to your kind. Most mortals would have turned back long ago. Cowardice has often proved to be the preferred option over certain demise, has it not? But you stayed. Perhaps there is hope for mankind yet."

But Evan didn't turn around. He was too captivated, wondering what news the locket held for Aegir.

"The locket revealed something important to your sister, Claire," said Ran, and Evan finally looked upon the goddess.

"Where is Claire?" Evan asked. "Is she all right? And how did the waves end up with her locket?"

"You ask many questions," said Ran with a sigh. "Do not fret; your sister is well. She and the others came to me, exclaiming they held some vital information. In good faith, your sister gave her locket to Himinglaeva, pleading with her to bring it to you."

"But why would Claire want for me to give Aegir the locket?"

"Are you not curious as to the nature of the locket's message?"

"Yes, of course."

Ran chuckled and said, "I will never understand humans, nor shall I ever truly favor them. It would seem, however, humans are not entirely at fault for the oil tanker spill in the Great Reef."

Ran paused and watched as her husband's expression changed from anger to concern. "One of our daughters was behind the poisoning of the Great Reef. It would seem Dufa created the wave that not only capsized that ship, but pushed it to the reef to make it look like humans were at fault."

"One of the waves did this?"

"Yes—Dufa. She is what you could consider our rogue wave."

"Why would she do something so horrible?"

"She has been angry at the humans for more than

159

a century. She wanted to punish mankind, but I never thought she would go this far. Once Aegir and I locate her, we will discover the reason behind her capsizing that ship."

"She's missing?" Evan asked. He studied the waves, surrounding Aegir. One, two, three … Ran was right; there were only eight waves. Where was Dufa?

"Yes, she is missing. Do not worry; most sea creatures are loyal to us. Dufa will be found very soon." Ran sighed and watched as her other eight daughters calmed the angry sea god. "I am glad Aegir was stopped before he flooded the entire planet. Mankind will be given another chance. Besides, I miss the grand festivities the Undersea Hall once held. I should very much like to have merpeople return, and perhaps a few selected humans."

Evan turned to look at the goddess. She winked and then gracefully wandered closer to the mountain's edge.

"Aegir might be a stern god, perhaps even irrational at times, but he has a good heart."

"I don't know what to say," said Evan. "Thanks for helping."

"In some respects, Lazonia is correct. Your kind is not a complete disappointment."

"I'm glad you feel that way."

"It is time to join your friends. Come with me."

Evan turned and realized he was standing on the ledge of a volcano.

"Whoa! I thought the Undersea Hall was under a mountain, not a volcano!" shouted Evan.

"Honestly, what difference does it make?"

"Don't volcanoes sometimes throw out scorching hot lava?"

"Of course they do. This volcano, however, erupts only when Aegir is *extremely* angry."

Evan looked back at Aegir and was relieved to see a smile on the sea god's face, as his daughters tugged playfully at his beard.

"I'll have to keep that in mind. I didn't want to upset him before, but now I definitely don't want to," said Evan.

"This volcano has been still for quite some time," said Ran. "In fact, I believe the last time this volcano erupted, a small island south of us sank. It caused quite a stir. I still do not see what all the fuss was about. The people of *that* particular island have thrived for thousands of years under the sea."

"You're not talking about Atlantis, are you?"

"Yes, that is its name. Aegir realized what his anger had done quickly enough and saved all of the island's inhabitants. But rarely does mankind tell stories about a god's sympathy. Typically, what is written is how this god reigned terror and that god turned poor little so-and-so into a terrible monster."

"So, those stories aren't true?" Evan asked.

"Yes, they are very true, at least most of them. What I am saying is that with every horrible story there are ten good ones."

"I suppose the same could be said for mankind," said Evan, and Ran stopped walking.

She stared at Evan for a moment before saying, "I am certain it could."

Evan shifted his attention back toward the volcano. Up ahead was a recess, big enough to hold a small car. From what Evan could see, it wasn't a tunnel. So, why was Ran leading him toward it? Evan didn't have to wonder for long when a large clamshell filled the space. It opened slowly and Ran motioned for Evan to go inside.

"I'm not so sure about this," said Evan.

"I assure you, it is safe. The Undersea Hall is very far below, and you will need to travel down many stories. Once inside, you will descend as if you were inside an elevator."

"So, it's a 'clam-o-vator'," said Evan while chuckling.

Ran smiled and nodded her head. Evan stepped inside the clam-o-vator and studied all of the golden buttons. Each one was stamped with a strange rune. Ran pressed her long finger onto the bottom one and the clam-o-vator descended smoothly.

Evan looked down and realized he still possessed the Serpent's Ring. Ran's eyes gazed upon the ring, but she did not try to take it.

"I'm not sure what I'm going to do with this," said Evan, rolling it around his wrist.

"I'm certain the professor will know," she advised. "If I were you, I would not flaunt it in front of my husband."

Evan nodded in agreement. He looked down, trying to figure out a safe place to put it. An idea came to him and he removed his shirt. He tore at the bottom of the sleeve and tied the Serpent's Ring to it. After putting his shirt back on, he tucked it away. For now, it was safely stored under the pit of his arm. Surely, nobody would want to search for it there.

Ran had been watching Evan and now smiled. "You are a clever boy, Evan Jones."

The clam-o-vator came to a smooth stop. In one efficient movement, the clam pivoted around and opened up. The seal widened, and Evan could see his sister and Lazonia.

"Evan!" Claire and Lazonia both cheered from the room beyond. It didn't take long for Dunkle and Barfel to leap up and dance on the table. Sigurd trailed behind the girls, smiling proudly. Evan entered the Undersea Hall once again, only this time, as a guest and not an intruder. Just as he walked toward his friends, he realized Ran was still in the clam-o-vator.

"Aren't you coming?" Evan asked curiously.

"I am afraid there is some unfinished business to which I must attend on the surface," answered Ran. "Besides, it would be best for you to have a private moment with your friends."

Evan smiled, and since he couldn't think of anything else to say, he said, "Thank you." She returned his smile as the door clamped shut.

Claire and Lazonia came forward and hugged Evan.

"I thought I told you not to do anything stupid!" scolded Claire as she released him.

"What were you thinking trying to confront Aegir all on your own?" chimed Lazonia.

"Perhaps you are a hero after all. Nice job. I cannot wait to hear the details," Sigurd said appraisingly, at which Claire looked startled.

"What he did was not heroic, it was dangerous. He's lucky to be alive," said Claire, narrowing her eyes.

"He is alive, and the world is safe. You underestimate him," returned Sigurd, and Evan felt his shoulders raise a little higher. Evan's opinion of this guy shot up exponentially.

Claire didn't respond. She gritted her teeth as she absorbed Sigurd's comment, and after a while, she looked at Evan.

"Fine, at least you're safe," said Claire, hugging him once more. She then whispered, "If you ever scare me like that again, I'll pummel you."

"No problem, Sis. I can honestly say my days of playing hero are over. Better left to guys like Sigurd."

Lazonia then wrapped her arms around Evan's waist and nuzzled her nose into his hair. He turned to her and beamed. Lazonia giggled and reached for his hand, leading him over to where the imps were frolicking on top of a table.

"Dunkle, I believe this belongs to you," said Evan, handing over the Serpent's Ring.

"If it is all the same to you, I would appreciate it if you could hold onto it for a little longer," said Dunkle. "You see, it has been a long time since I was able to join in the merrymaking of my fellow imps."

"But, there are only two imps here," said Evan, staring over at Barfel.

"For now, yes; however, tomorrow the Undersea Hall will be swarming with imps," said Dunkle with an ever-growing smile.

Suddenly, a concerned voice filled the entire room, "Lazonia!" It was Ragnar, who was obviously delighted to find her unharmed, but now upset by her disappearance.

"It looks as if I need a moment with my father," she said and rushed over.

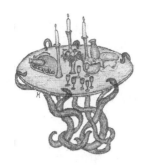

Chapter Twenty-Five

FEAST AND FOLLY

EVAN WATCHED FROM ACRISS THE room, as Lazonia spoke with Ragnar. The merman's tail had become legs. And although his arms and chest were bare, gold leaf wrapped around his waist and down to his ankles.

More merpeople appeared through the elaborate entranceway, and they eventually filled the room; their newly formed legs were covered with multicolored gems. Music floated through the Undersea Hall. Laughter and cheer erupted from table to table. Lazonia had been successful at calming her upset father, and even though Evan sat far away, he could tell Ragnar's spirits had lifted.

Sigurd and Claire were across the table from Evan, who was forced to overhear their ridiculous sweetie-talk. Dunkle and Barfel were far more entertaining. They clambered along tabletops, leaping onto the long wooden benches, and then bounding along the floor, the aroma of pine and cedar trailing behind.

All of a sudden, a strange breeze wafted through the Undersea Hall. Mist streamed in from another hallway. Lazonia's friend, Himinglaeva, emerged from a faint cloud, her body forming from miniscule droplets. The two raced to each other and embraced. Evan knew it had been a long time since either had been friendly to one another. Now, they giggled as if no time had passed.

"Welcome back, old friends," erupted Aegir, but he was still nowhere in sight.

Those in the Undersea Hall quieted and turned their attention to the center of the room. Water drizzled down from above. In perfect unison, they took the form of Aegir. Although his hair was the same dark black with turquoise-blue streaks from before, his height was now substantially shorter—about eight feet.

"The Undersea Hall has been empty for far too long," Aegir's voice reverberated around the entire room. "Let us celebrate our friendship. Enjoy yourselves."

His speech was brief, and Evan knew there was more to say, but that could wait until tomorrow. He watched Ragnar and Aegir approach each other and felt the warmth emanating from their reunion.

"This is how it should be," whispered Lazonia from behind Evan.

"I have to admit, while I was on that cliff, Aegir scared me half to death. But now, seeing him in here, I understand him a little better," said Evan, as he continued to watch Ragnar and Aegir.

"You must be starving," said Lazonia. "Come on, let's eat."

In all his fourteen years, Evan had never eaten food like this: dulse-cakes with lemon hollandaise sauce, roasted wakame, bladderwack bisque. He even tried the kombu Rockefeller (not served over fish). Each delicacy was unbelievable! And the best part was that each time he finished his plate, more elaborate seafare appeared.

Somewhat camouflaged by their transparent skin, Evan barely noticed the inconspicuous squidlike men as they removed the empty plates and replaced them with new platters of food. Evan watched as one of the squid men approached him. He had unsettling eyes bulging out from the sides of his spade-shaped head. Squid Man lifted another empty plate with ease by using one of his tentacles, and in one solid movement, used another roving arm to set down five drinks. Evan had to admit, these servers where incredibly efficient.

"This room's only purpose is to host celebrations," explained Lazonia. "It has been that way for thousands of years."

"I'm not used to seeing food being served by squid men. Don't get me wrong, I don't have a problem with it. It's just ... different," said Evan, shoving another stuffed sea-grape leaf into his mouth.

Although activity in the room was constant, Evan couldn't stop watching Aegir. If the sea god wasn't seated at the round table, he was busy greeting his guests. His boisterous laughter was louder than anything else. For the most part, Ran was at his side. All traces of loneliness had faded from her eyes. And when she peered over at Evan, she smiled brightly. She whispered into Aegir's ear and now he too was staring at Evan.

Amidst the celebrations, the sea god and his wife stood up from their chairs, and with mighty steps, walked over to Evan. He didn't realize it, but he had slouched down so low, he was almost under the table.

"Evan, what are you doing?" said Lazonia, lifting his arm. "You said it yourself, Aegir is not so bad."

"That was when he was across the room!" said Evan anxiously. "Why are they coming over here?"

"Do you really have to ask? Now, do not be rude. Sit up and calm down."

Evan tried to sit straight and forced the corners of his lips to turn up. What would Evan say to the sea god?

"It would seem I was mildly harsh in my sentence for mankind," said Aegir. "Our daughter may have been behind this mess, but I can assure you mankind has

167

done his share of damage to my oceans."

Evan spoke not a word. He held himself frozen like a statue, realizing this would be a terrible time for sarcasm. Aegir and Ran sat down, and Aegir folded his hands, placing them on the table. The god's demeanor was casual, as if he and Evan were old friends.

Aegir sighed before saying, "Young man, you stood your ground. It was exceptionally brave of you to battle against a god."

"Thanks," said Evan, looking toward his feet.

"Evan, please look up," said Ran. "What my husband is trying to say is you have aided in giving mankind another chance. You have done well. If it had not been for your determination, we might never have known the truth about Dufa."

"What now?" asked Evan. "What will you do to her?"

"There is little I can do, until I find her," stated Aegir, shrugging his shoulders.

"But, what if she tries to blame mankind for something else?"

"Dufa will be dealt with," said Ran. "I can assure you of that."

"Well, that isn't very reassuring," said Evan.

"Mankind will live to see another day," said Aegir. "That will have to suffice."

"Oh, and you should retire soon. You have had a busy day, and tomorrow the real banquet begins. Many more will arrive," said Ran.

Evan peered around the grand hall. The long rectangular tables were already filled with merpeople.

"Does this room stretch?" he wondered aloud.

"You will see, the Undersea Hall is able to accommodate its guests," said Ran, rising from the table. Before leaving she added, "You will be glad to hear that Dr. Irving and Vor will be here in the morning. Now, rest well."

As if on cue, Himinglaeva arrived. Jubilantly, she

danced across the floor. "Are you ready?" she asked, sounding much like the rush of a wave.

"For what?" Evan questioned.

"I am playing hostess and will show you to your room," she answered gracefully and twirled. "It would appear your imps are enjoying themselves."

"Yes, they like to party, even when they aren't at a party," said Evan, watching Dunkle and Barfel hop from place to place.

"They are restless and seem to have energy to spare," said Himinglaeva, studying the imps. "They may stay. As for the four of you, please follow me."

"I guess we don't have a choice here," Claire whispered to Evan as they were led away from the celebration.

Himinglaeva moved much like a wave rolls over the ocean's surface. Lazonia joined her friend, and the two proceeded to gossip about the latest mishaps that had just occurred in the Undersea Hall.

They entered a long, cavelike corridor. Immediately, the live-eel wall sconces sizzled and sparkled with electric light. Tiny crabs and other creatures dashed in and out of holes. Pits were everywhere—along the wall, the floor, and the ceiling. Evan watched the buglike crustaceans scurry around.

"Yuck. I hope our room doesn't come with live sea creatures," said Evan, still shivering.

Lazonia laughed and said, "Your room will come equipped with a hammock, making it a little more difficult for crabs to visit you in your sleep."

The group reached Evan's room, and as the others waited in the hallway, Lazonia led him inside.

"See you tomorrow," said Lazonia, squeezing him tight.

"Are you sure this place is safe?" whispered Evan.

"See you tomorrow ... my hero," she said and pulled away.

He sighed and then walked into the strange room. The first thing he noticed was that it smelled like sea salt. The walls and floor looked like the inside of a shell, pearlescent and polished. Whereas most of the room's surface was light in color and smooth, the far corner was drastically different—it was colorful, looking much like living coral. Water trickled down in that area, creating a basin at the bottom, and shells were embedded in the floor.

There were no windows and no television. There was nothing for Evan to do but sleep. Wearily, he rinsed his body in the pooling water and then climbed onto the golden hammock. The room slowly faded from dim light to a mild darkness. A soft breeze circulated, and the hammock swayed, cradling Evan into a delicious slumber.

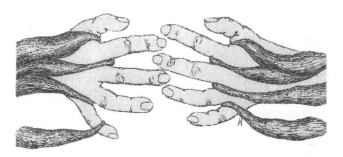

CHAPTER TWENTY-SIX

COME DROWN WITH ME

A s Evan's thoughts drifted, dreams clamored for his attention. He stood on the cliff, begging Aegir to reconsider. Only this time, when Aegir turned, it was not the sea god's face Evan saw. Someone else was trying to unlock Jormundgand.

"Who are you?" screamed Evan.

"Alamaz ..." whispered the man, and then he was gone. A girl rose up out of one of the waves, and although her back was to Evan, he could see her body emerging from the sea foam. The Serpent's Ring continued to rise, and Jormundgand was tumultuous.

"What are you doing?" Evan asked the girl, but she ignored him.

Something wrapped around his chest, and he was pulled back, hard against pitted rocks!

He sat upright in his hammock. And although he could breathe, his lungs felt squeezed.

"That dream felt a little too real," said Evan, his hand clenching his chest.

171

In the dim blue light, he could see the room hadn't changed. He climbed out of the hammock, and his foot landed on the floor. It was wet. He could hear the faint sound of rushing water, flooding into his room. He leapt off the hammock and raced for the door. But the water rose quickly and was soon up to his waist. Something wrapped around his chest and pulled him under! Evan fought, thrusting and kicking his legs.

Under the water, a girl's voice asked, "Where is the Serpent's Ring?"

Evan was released and rushed to the surface. The space between his head and ceiling was getting smaller. "Where are you? Show yourself," gasped Evan.

"Where is the Serpent's Ring?"

Evan didn't answer, and again, she dragged him down. He searched, but all he saw was gushing water. Finally, a pale-faced girl came forth. She reminded Evan of Himinglaeva, with her pearly skin and beautiful features. But this girl's expression was a lot less friendly. Her eyes narrowed, and her mouth snarled. She shook him violently, plunging him deeper into the water.

Evan thrashed around, until at last, his head erupted up into a small pocket of air. Again, he struggled for breath.

"I asked one simple question, and you will answer! Where is the Serpent's Ring?" she shrilled from below.

"Why do you want the Serpent's Ring?"

She didn't answer. She yanked him down again, and this time, his back slammed against the floor! All of his reserve air shot out of his lungs. He couldn't breathe; he was done for. What a fool he had been to believe he had succeeded on his quest.

Evan lay motionless, waiting for her to attack him again. She grabbed him by the neck and rushed him to the surface. He breathed in the salty air, wondering why she didn't just end him.

"Think of the consequences," Evan mumbled. "Your father does not want to flood the planet anymore."

The water level dropped a little. A few inches away, sea foam sizzled and from it a girl's head emerged. The ninth sister circled around Evan, glaring, her icy stare making him shiver.

"You have absolutely no idea who you are dealing with," she said. "I am a daughter of Aegir and Ran, rulers of the sea. I am the wave Dufa. I have lived for thousands of years. And you are Evan, a young, naïve boy."

"Yes, that's true. But just so you know, I will not give you the Serpent's Ring. In fact, it's not even in this room."

"You are a liar! I will find what I am after. It matters nothing to me whether or not you are alive to assist me."

"Then you are going to have to let me drown. I will not help."

"So be it!"

Water surged over Evan's head, and he felt a mighty tug. Again, his body was slammed onto a hard surface. He twisted and turned. What could he do? There must be something. He thought and thought until an idea came to him. He concentrated and tried to push the water back. Nothing happened; the entire room was full with water. He needed to get the water out, but how?

The door! Cautiously, he used his mental powers to turn the door's handle. Slowly and carefully, he imagined he was releasing the lock. It worked! The door swung toward the hallway, and water spilled out. Evan knelt on the floor, coughing and sputtering. When he tried to stand, he was whacked on the back. Pain spread from his head down to his knees. He fell forward and tried to regain his strength. He tried to stand, but again, he felt something wallop him.

Abruptly, Dufa's long fingers stretched, encircling his neck! He reached back to grab her, but his hands simply passed through water. He concentrated on the hammock and swung it at Dufa. It wrapped around her watery body, but it flowed right through her. Evan's options were running low, and again, he was knocked to the ground.

Water suddenly splashed above, beside and around him. Dufa and Himinglaeva struggled against one another. More waves arrived, all battling against their rogue sister.

An arm grasped Evan, yanking him out of the turbulence. He landed in the hallway, safe. It was Lazonia.

"Are you all right?" Lazonia asked, kneeling down to his level.

"Yeah, I think so," said Evan.

"I heard commotion from your room. I am so sorry. I really thought you would be safe in there."

"This wasn't your fault," he said, gripping his battered side.

"Evan!" Claire's voice rang from a few feet away. "What happened? You look terrible."

"Dufa … the missing wave … tried to kill me," Evan said in between gasps. "Apparently … she doesn't agree with Aegir's new plan … she wants the Serpent's Ring."

"Is the Serpent's Ring safe?" Sigurd asked, still approaching.

"Yeah … it's right here," Evan said and removed the Serpent's Ring from inside his shirt.

"I'm just glad you're all right," said Claire, hugging him.

"Ow, I wouldn't exactly say I was all right. She banged me up pretty good," said Evan, wincing.

A furious Aegir thundered down the hall. "What is the meaning of this? How could Dufa continue to go against my wishes?"

"I am certain she believed she was following through with your wishes, Dear," said Ran diplomatically.

"My wishes have changed!" yelled Aegir.

"For years, you have complained about how mankind has ruined your oceans. I am sure Dufa feels as strongly against man as you do."

"You dare to say this is my fault?" questioned Aegir, stopping right in front of Evan.

"In some respects, yes, I do. She is always trying to gain your attention," said Ran calmly.

"Perhaps, you are right," Aegir said and looked down. "What have I done?"

"There is time to fix this problem," said Ran, placing a hand on Aegir's shoulder.

"You are correct," Aegir said and looked at Evan. "We will discuss the terms of our peaceful resolution tomorrow."

With that, the sea god whisked past Evan and stormed into the room. Ran was right behind him, whispering rational words of advice. From where he sat, Evan could hear Aegir howl in another language, and then the splashing water halted. The door slammed shut, and Evan was relieved he was not on its other side.

"I really don't want to talk with him," admitted Evan.

"Do not worry," said Lazonia. "Gods generally do not discuss anything for long. They get to the point—very short and very brief."

"Well, let's hope. The less time I have to spend with Aegir, the better," said Evan, looking up at his bedroom door. "I wonder how long they'll be arguing in my room."

"Why don't you stay in my room tonight?" volunteered Claire. "I'll keep an eye on you."

"Thanks," strained Evan, as he attempted to stand. "I'm exhausted."

Sigurd rushed to his aid, "Here, let me help."

Evan managed to travel the short, painful journey to Claire's room.

"Hey, this room's nicer than my room. What gives?"

175

said Evan, upon entering her suite.

"I'm a teenage girl. I need more space, along with all of the other creature comforts," rationalized Claire. "Evan, you can stay in the room over there."

"I only had one room. How many rooms are in here?" said Evan.

"I don't know, a few," said Claire, leading Evan and Sigurd through a living room of sorts.

"There's a TV?" Evan asked, noticing a few of Claire's extra amenities.

"Of course, didn't you have one?" said Claire.

"No, I didn't."

"Well, the shows are a little unusual. If it weren't for the subtitles, I'd have no idea what anyone was talking about," said Claire. "There's this one show with three mermaids. It's very good."

"Oh, I love that show," exclaimed Lazonia.

"Come on, I'll help you get situated," offered Sigurd, as he helped Evan onto the hammock. Once settled, Lazonia and Claire were swiftly at his side.

"What can I get for you?" Claire asked.

"A towel would be nice," mumbled Evan.

"On it!" said Claire, dashing out the door.

"It has been a very long time since I have seen a television," Sigurd said with a smile, leaving Evan alone with *his* mermaid.

"I cannot believe Dufa tried to kill you," said Lazonia.

"Let me guess: she was always the sweet one," chided Evan.

"No, she has always been aggressive. After all, her name means to dive."

"That doesn't surprise me. She tossed me around pretty efficiently," Evan said with a weak smile.

"Of all the sisters, Dufa would be the one wanting to see Aegir's plan through. Once she gets an idea in her thick head, that is." After finding a small cloth, Lazonia

176

wiped it over Evan's brow.

"Well, I wouldn't want to be her right now. Aegir looked really angry."

"One thing is for certain, Dufa will be dealt with."

"Lazonia, there's one other thing that has been bothering me." Evan sighed and looked away. "Just before Dufa tried to drown me, I had another nightmare."

"And?"

"Alamaz was there, trying to unlock Jormundgand, but I'm sure it's nothing. Right?"

"Let us hope it is nothing, but I will discuss this with Aegir ... just in case."

CHAPTER TWENTY-SEVEN

NOT AGAIN

EVAN SLEPT WELL THAT NIGHT, having happy dreams instead of nightmares.

"It's time to wake up, Sleeping Beauty," said Claire, as she poured water into Evan's cup. "It's almost noon. I'm pretty impressed with myself for resisting the urge to wake you earlier."

"I slept that long? I guess I was really tired," grunted Evan.

"Yeah, you hardly moved."

"Thanks for watching over me."

"No prob. But you need to get up. There are a few people who would like to see you. And you won't believe this one; it looks like Alamaz *was* behind Dufa's extreme behavior!"

"Alamaz? You mean that immortal guy who tried to steal the Mysticus from the gods—that Alamaz?"

"You know more than I gave you credit for," Claire said with a smile.

"But I thought he was locked up in nightmares or something."

"From what I understand, even though Alamaz has been trapped inside the Dungeon of Dreadful Dreams,

178

he is still able to communicate with some creatures."

"You mean to tell me, Alamaz is still in the picture?"

"Yes, it turns out he corrupted Dufa through her dreams. He convinced her to capsize the ship over the Great Reef," said Claire, wandering to a chair shaped like a clamshell. She lifted a pile of nicely folded clothes and returned to Evan. "Here, Himinglaeva brought these for you." With that, Claire tossed them onto her immobile brother. "And look, there's a pair of shoes under the chair."

"Finally, I can wear sneakers again," said Evan, staring at the brown leather flip-flops. "Those aren't really my style; could you maybe change them into sneakers?"

"When in Rome, Evan. When in Rome," said Claire.

"I suppose that means you won't change them."

"No."

Evan lifted the shirt to his face and inhaled—fresh, white cotton. It had been days since he had worn anything remotely clean.

"I see you also have some new clothes," Evan said upon noticing his sister's white dress.

Claire stood in front of the mirror, admiring her reflection. Her dress wrapped around her neck, scooped down in the back, and draped to her feet.

"Sigurd thinks I look like a goddess," she sighed. "And look, these pearls are real."

And so they were. Pearls lined the straps and bottom trim.

"It's nice," said Evan.

"Well, got to go. Sigurd's waiting for me in the Undersea Hall," she said and fluttered away. "Make sure you try the sea salt bath, it will heal anything," she hollered back to him.

"Don't worry about me. I don't need any help getting out of this hammock or anything," mumbled Evan, trying to sit upright. Carefully, he edged his legs over and slid to the floor. His entire body ached, and although he wanted to crawl, he managed to stumble over to the bathing area.

"How is this supposed to help?" wondered Evan, staring at the circular pool.

He crept into the shallow edge. As soon as he had both feet in, something started to fizz. Small bubbles whizzed around the saucerlike tub, and water massaged his aching muscles.

"This is going to be interesting," said Evan, sliding deeper into the warm salt bath.

After Evan stepped out of the tub, he put on his new outfit. Definitely not like anything he would wear at home, but at least the clothes were clean. The tuniclike shirt hung down too low, and the pants were way too baggy. And he never wore flip-flops. In the end, he didn't care if he looked like a geek, the cotton was exceptionally soft against his skin, and that was all that mattered.

He wandered down the long, barnacle-covered tunnel toward the Undersea Hall. As he neared the Hall, he was shocked by how loud it was inside. He wondered just how many people Ran had invited and couldn't believe they were already in celebration mode so early in the afternoon.

A few feet ahead, one of the Undersea Hall's smaller entrances came into view. Two large gilded eels wrapped around the opening. Evan watched, as their eyes followed him.

"Creepy," said Evan, ducking a little lower.

From inside the Undersea Hall, more than a thousand merpeople, gods, and a variety of other creatures gathered. Every single one of them stared at Evan and the room fell silent. After a moment, a great applause ensued. He looked to his left and right and behind. He was the only one standing there, and all eyes were focused on him.

"Evan Jones!" said Aegir with his mighty voice. "Come, stand before those who wish to thank you."

Evan inched his way to where Aegir stood. In truth, Evan was more terrified of all this new attention than he was of Jormundgand.

"You are a true hero," said Aegir, patting Evan on the shoulder. "I believe this belongs to you."

Dangling from his enormous hand, hung the divining locket. Evan reached for it and said, "Actually, it belongs to my sister. Thanks."

"Make sure it finds its rightful owner. We would not want an all seeing locket to fall into the hands of Alamaz," said Aegir before walking away.

Evan hadn't moved yet, when from the corner of his eye he saw a flash of violet hair. "Come, join us," encouraged Lazonia. "Today, we celebrate your heroism. And tomorrow they will come up with another excuse to gather."

"Do they party every single day?" Evan asked.

"They do on most days, yes."

They approached the table right next to where twenty-five or more imps danced, each one a different color with variations in their markings. All of them had hair that stood straight up, forming fuzzy mohawks. And it smelled to Evan like he had entered a forest.

Claire and Sigurd sat with Dr. Irving and Vor. They were in the middle of a discussion, and by the look on Claire's face it was a fascinating one at that.

"So, there I was, innocently bathing under a waterfall. How was I to know it was the secret entrance to Vor's dwellings?" said Dr. Irving, laughing so hard he had to wipe away a tear.

"Imagine, if you will, my surprise at finding this

human using my waterfall as his personal shower. Well, that did not please me. Not one tiny bit!" said Vor.

"What did you do?" Claire asked eagerly.

"Of course, I hid his clothing," answered Vor, laughing along with the group.

"Once I realized the error of my ways, I promised never to insult Vor, or any other goddess, like that again," added Dr. Irving.

"Needless to say, he made it up to me," said Vor, running her fingers through the professor's hair.

"How did he manage that?" Claire asked.

"I did what any other love-struck man would. Every day, I brought her flowers and laid them outside her waterfall," said Dr. Irving.

"That is so sweet," said Claire, lightly resting her chin on top of her hand.

"That was not all he brought. Eventually, he added razzleberries. And that is how he won my forgiveness and my heart," added Vor.

"So, when did you decide to stay here to be with Vor?" Claire asked.

"That decision was made the instant I met her," said Dr. Irving.

"Why did you decide to stay here? I mean, why not have Vor live in our world?" Claire asked, briefly glancing at Sigurd.

"My dear girl, it is forbidden for gods and goddesses to leave Sagaas," said Vor, and she too glanced at Sigurd. "Normally, it is forbidden for immortals to permanently leave, as well."

"Have there been any exceptions? Has an immortal ever lived in Terra?" Claire asked hopefully.

"I am afraid it is not time to reveal information of that nature to you, dear," said Vor.

"Claire, I will visit you," said Sigurd, draping his arm down around her waist.

"And you may keep the divining locket. Use it as a way to communicate with each other and me," said Vor.

"That's right, Claire, here's your locket," interrupted Evan. "Aegir returned it to me."

"Thanks," said Claire, her eyes welling up.

Evan looked at Lazonia and felt a twinge in his heart. For the first time in his life, he felt empathy for his sister.

Evan hesitated before asking, "Vor, will we be able to come back?"

As if waiting for permission to answer, Vor glanced at Dr. Irving, who nodded his head.

"You will return. Your adventures in Sagaas are not over," announced Vor. "But, I will say no more."

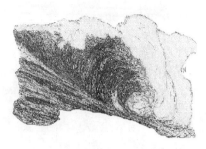

CHAPTER TWENTY-EIGHT

SURF'S UP, DUDE

BY EARLY EVENING, THE CELEBRATION was in full swing. Twenty or more imps controlled the floor. They hopped and cheered and occasionally created a giant circle, where they snapped their tails into its center, looped them around each other, and continued to dance in rings.

Sigurd and Claire had quietly shuffled off to the side. They danced to their own slow rhythm. Lazonia was being entertained by another of Himinglaeva's sisters, and Dr. Irving and Vor had been joined by a god with wild, yellow hair, which actually moved around, all by itself.

Evan feasted alone, relishing in the quiet moment. It gave him a minute to absorb all that had happened, and as he picked at his grilled sea lettuce with "Seasar" dressing, he wondered how he would be able to resume a normal life.

"You will be surprised by how easy it will be," said Vor, joining his thoughts.

"How did you know what I was ..." and Evan realized quickly the reason she understood. "I sometimes forget that you're the goddess who knows everything."

184

"I suspect there is something you wish to ask."

"Why me? Why was I the one to go on this quest?"

"After all you have accomplished, you still doubt yourself," she stated, and Evan shrugged. Vor sighed, and continued, "I do not understand this weakness in humans. You question yourselves far too much."

"Sure we do, sometimes. Don't you ever question yourself?"

"No," said Vor abruptly. "Gods might not always make the right decisions, but at least we make them with conviction. Even when we are wrong, we are right."

"I noticed Aegir still doesn't act like he did anything wrong. He seems to believe what he did was right. He probably thinks because everyone is together again that he did something noble, when it was his fault everyone split ways in the first place," realized Evan.

"Correct. What happened, happened. There is nothing anyone can do about the past, including Aegir. He will embrace his mistake and treat it as though now the world were a better place for it."

"Why did I have all of those dreams about Aegir's sharks and waves before I took the Serpent's Ring? Somehow I fit into this puzzle, and I'm not sure how or why," said Evan.

"You wonder if you were preselected for this quest."

"Yeah, I guess."

"Everyone must follow his own destiny and is chosen for some sort of quest. Yours happened to lead you here. And the answers are meant to come to you along the way. What is important, now, is that you pushed through your fear and doubt. Yes, you have been connected to Sagaas, all along. But, I must not say anymore. You will find answers to your questions in days yet to come." She stood to leave, adding, "Evan, pay special attention to what your dreams are showing you. There is almost always a message hidden in them. You must also be careful; Alamaz will try to corrupt you through your nightmares."

"Why do you think Alamaz wants to flood Terra?"

"I might have all knowing power, however, I tend to find the dream world a bit confusing. Since Alamaz lives in the dream world, I have trouble 'seeing' him clearly. I can only speculate to his reasoning."

"Well, what do you think?"

"Alamaz has always been jealous of the gods' powers. That is why, many thousands of years ago, he tried to steal the Mysticus Orb. Now that he is trapped in the Dungeon of Dreadful Dreams, I believe he wants to claim power from the relics."

"So, he can escape."

"Yes, and not only does he want to escape, if Alamaz were to find all of the relics, he would become unimaginably powerful."

"What will the gods do to stop him?"

"All those in Sagaas will keep a watchful eye on Alamaz, but like I said, he is very cunning and manipulative."

"So, we have to wait and see what he does next?"

"I am afraid so," said Vor with a smile. "It might comfort you to know that I will be watching over you and your sister. I have been for a long time now."

"I appreciate that," said Evan. "Thanks."

Vor ran her fingers under Evan's chin and then wandered back toward Dr. Irving.

Again, Evan was alone. He looked around for Lazonia. She was still laughing along with some of the waves. Sigurd and Claire appeared to enjoy their "private" moment, and Dunkle and Barfel would probably dance the night away. Maybe Ran was right; for now at least, life was good.

⌁⌁⌁

Early the next morning, Evan stood on a pure-white, sandy beach. There were tiny ripples, lapping along the shore. The sun was bright, and Evan soaked in its rays. After spending many days underwater, he vowed to spend more of his time away from video games and explore outdoors more often.

"Glorious, isn't it?" said Lazonia, who had joined him. "Over the past few months, I have spent most of my time hiding underwater. I greatly missed the sunlight."

"I can imagine you normally spend your days sitting on a rock, near a waterfall, brushing your hair with a blowfish," teased Evan, and Lazonia playfully swatted his arm.

"You have never surfed properly, unless you have made friends with the waves," she said, staring at the calm sea.

"Do you like to surf?"

"Why do you look so surprised?" Lazonia asked. "Do you want for me to show you how mermaids surf? We have some time. The others are still chatting inside."

Evan nodded his head yes, kicked off his flip-flops, and dashed into the calm ocean. Water circled his ankles, and it felt like a lukewarm bath.

"A little anxious, are we?" shouted Lazonia, still standing on shore. "I need to call Himinglaeva. We won't be able to surf without her and her sister Hefring. They will make the water rise into a wave."

Careful not to touch the water, Lazonia cupped her hands around her face. A soft breeze came from her open mouth and skimmed over the surface. It rushed past Evan and arched down into the sea.

"What was that?" said Evan, still staring at the place where the wake ended.

"I just placed a call, of course."

Before Evan could blink, Lazonia leapt head first through the air. She sliced through the water, and with a flick of her tail, she was gone.

"Hey, where did you go?" hollered Evan, spinning around and around. He was facing the shore, when something from behind erupted with a loud rush. He turned quickly and saw, from the still water, a great wave arose. And there was Lazonia, skimming along with it. Her tail barely visible, as her upper body shot through the wave's barrel.

"Are you ready?" came a whisper. Evan looked around, but didn't see anyone.

Suddenly, water rose up around his waist. With a mighty splash, Himinglaeva appeared, giggling.

"Whoa, you startled me," said Evan, grasping at his racing heart.

"Sorry, I could not help myself," laughed Himinglaeva. "Would you like to surf?"

"I'd love to, but I don't exactly know how."

"I will be there to give you a little nudge when it is time to stand."

"But, I don't have a surfboard."

"You can body surf."

"That's not the same thing."

"Now, swim to just over there," she said and disappeared.

He swam out and waited and waited.

"What am I supposed to do, now?" he asked, but the wave had vanished.

"Evan, what are you doing out there?" yelled Claire, approaching with Sigurd.

"I'm about to catch a wave," grunted Evan, trying not to look ridiculous.

"There aren't any waves. And you don't have a surfboard," she said, shaking her head. "I'll take your word for it. Here," she said and created a surfboard out of some driftwood. She slid it toward Evan, who directed it his way.

"Thanks!" he said after catching it. "Can you make one like this for me at home?"

Evan heard some gurgling, and then the water near him rose up ten feet high. It didn't roll forward. It just continued to rush upward, forming into an ideal wave.

Lazonia appeared off to his side. "Lie down on the board and paddle!"

Water surged forward with his body, lifting him. He felt an extra nudge into the back of his legs. He popped up; his feet were steady on the board. "Water hands" held him in place, helping him gain balance. He positioned his feet like he had seen surfers do on TV and stuck out his arms. The wave traveled toward the shore, and when it was still a little ways out, it stopped going forward. Evan was surfing the endless wave.

"Don't think. Allow your body to relax," instructed Lazonia, appearing beside him, moving along the crest.

Evan let go, released his thoughts, and coasted along the pipeline.

"Looking good!" yelled Claire.

"This is epic!" shouted Evan.

"Evan, let's see if you can do this," Lazonia hollered from the other side of the tube. She skimmed along, rushing to the wave's lip. She took off into the air, using the wave as a ramp.

"Sure, you can do that because you have a tail, and you're body surfing. It's different on a board," declared Evan, safely maneuvering along, traveling up and down.

"You have to try it," said Lazonia. "Himinglaeva, rush him up the wave!"

"No, no, that's all right ... Whoa!" And he was swept up the arc and shot into air.

Exhilarating, thrilling, breathtaking! He didn't want to come back down. So, he didn't. He held himself up above the wave, controlling the board with his mental powers. He twisted and flipped, barely even touching the crest.

"Now, you're just showing off," Lazonia teased and splashed water at him.

He laughed and stumbled a bit, but he didn't crash down; the wave cradled him as he fell. Slowly, the water became flat and calm. Two wave-girls emerged from sea foam: Himinglaeva and her sister, Hefring.

"Thanks. That was insane," said Evan.

"No problem. May I keep the board?" Himinglaeva asked, and Evan slid the board over to her. "Thank you, Evan. I am going to try this. It looked like a lot of fun."

"An experience I'll never forget," Evan said and trudged for the beach.

CHAPTER TWENTY-NINE

FLY AWAY HOME

"I HAVE TO ADMIT, YOU HAVE skills, little bro," said Claire, as Evan reached the shore.

"Who knew, right? I don't suppose you have a towel handy?" Evan asked, shaking water from his hair.

"No, sorry," shrugged Claire.

"Ah, it's alright. I'll air dry."

Dunkle and Barfel bounded along, kicking up the sand. They were followed by Aegir and Ran, and behind them came a long trail of people.

"Is *everyone* coming to see us off?" Evan whispered to Claire.

"I'm pretty sure they are," she replied.

It didn't take long for the large group to congregate. Evan tried to calculate just how many had arrived. He was tired of all the attention and had hoped for a quiet send off. But that apparently wasn't going to happen.

"Sigurd, I have a surprise for you. A gift from Evan and me," announced Claire. Sheepishly, she glanced over at Evan, who smiled. She led Sigurd closer to the shoreline and pointed toward the horizon. "Sigurd, watch over there. Evan, are you ready?"

Evan nodded and focused. A large area of water

191

rumbled, and a warm glow materialized from below. A golden fin broke the surface. Eventually, the entire gilded whale-pod emerged. Claire stepped forward and gracefully waved her arms. As Evan held the gilded whale up in the air, Claire transfigured it into a giant sphere, rapidly spinning on its axis. With apparent ease, she stretched out the ball, forming it into a great Viking ship. As Evan carefully returned the gilded boat to water, it continued to spin around.

"It might not be enchanted, but it's made from real gold. Do you think you can track dragons in it?" Claire asked.

"Are you offering me the use of this vessel?" questioned Sigurd.

"Yes, it's yours. Evan and I can't exactly take home a ship made from gold; too many questions would be asked," she said casually.

Sigurd lifted Claire and spun her around, her feet swinging in air. She giggled like a lovesick puppy, and Evan rolled his eyes. Eventually, Sigurd set her down and placed a kiss on her forehead.

"Thank you. I believe it will serve me well," Sigurd said and turned to Evan. "And thank you, Evan. I wondered how I was going to be able to sail the seas without a ship."

"No problem," said Evan. "I guess since we left our glass ship back on the island of giants, we had better make something else for us to travel home in. Come to think of it, should we go back for our ship?"

"Please, allow me to take care of it for you," offered Sigurd.

"What will you do with it?" Claire asked.

"I will offer it to the giants, to bargain for peace and safe passage onto their island. You would not believe how difficult it is to trap dragons while also being hunted by giants."

"I'm glad it'll help you," said Claire, staring at the sand. She then lifted her arms. "Okay, I better make another glass ship."

"Wait, wait!" yelled Dr. Irving, scuttling closer to Claire and Evan. "There is a better way to travel home."

"Should we create another submarine?" Evan asked curiously.

"No, no. You two have not yet discovered the full depth of your powers," said Dr. Irving. "Please, allow me to demonstrate."

With that, he stepped back and raised his arms. He lowered them, and along with his movements, feathers sprouted out from his entire body. His arms transformed into wings, and his legs morphed into talons. He now had piercing eyes, a sharp beak, and a tail made up of red-brown feathers edged with white. He was an oversize hawk!

"Whoa, one of us can do that?" Evan asked.

"Yes, I believe the person with the power of transfiguration will be able to," Dr. Irving said, looking at Claire.

"I can change us into an animal?" said Claire, sounding both shocked and amazed.

"Yes, you should be able to. And there is something else I need to say before you leave," began Dr. Irving. "Use your powers wisely, especially once you are home."

"You mean we get to keep them?" Evan asked in awe. And the professor nodded. Evan continued excitedly, "I guess I hadn't thought about whether we'd still have them once we were home."

"Do not use them in front of others. Humans might not be able to see the magic you perform, but they will be able to see the results," added Dr. Irving.

"I don't understand. People won't be able to see us use our powers?" Evan asked.

"No. Not unless you wish for them to. Magic should

not be seen by mortals, nor should anything related to Sagaas. For example, your parents would not be able to see Dunkle, unless he allowed them. And if you use your power to say, throw a rock, then your parents would see the rock in its new location but have no idea how it got there."

"What if we changed ourselves into birds? What would they see?" Claire asked.

"Again, unless you allowed them to see you in bird form, they would see you in your human body," said Dr. Irving. "And if you speak about your time here in Asgard, they will not hear a word you are saying. They will not even see your lips move. The gods were very careful when they decided to hide Sagaas from mankind."

"Awesome," said Evan, looking at Claire. "What are you going to change us into? How about a dragon or something? That would be cool."

Claire said nothing. She stood motionless as if pondering Evan's question. "I suppose I could turn us into dolphins or something."

"I would recommend flying; your journey back would be much faster and less tiresome," advised Dr. Irving.

"Right," Claire said and looked down at Dunkle and Barfel. "Do you have any thoughts about what you would like to turn into?"

"I agree with Evan: a dragon would be rather nice," said Dunkle. "But, I suppose it does not really matter, as long as we once again return to our imp form."

"All right, I think I know what to do," said Claire. "Don't move. I don't want to mess this up."

"Wait a minute!" interjected Evan. "Maybe Dr. Irving should change us. I mean, no offense, but Claire doesn't really know what she's doing."

"Claire will be fine, Evan," said Dr. Irving, still in his hawk form.

Evan continued to stare at the professor, marveling

at how strange it was to hear his proper English accent come from the beak of a human-size bird. Indeed, Evan was so mesmerized he hardly noticed when giant wings started to emerge from his own back.

"So, you decided to manipulate your own DNA and added wings to your human form. Very nicely done, Claire," appraised Dr. Irving.

"I have wings!" declared Evan, stretching his neck to better see his new black feathers.

Dunkle and Barfel had become imps with wings. Dunkle's wings matched his greenish-blue body and Barfel's were red-orange. They too were admiring each other's new wings.

"You look like an angel," said Sigurd while approaching Claire.

Evan looked her way and noticed that she sort of did. She was still wearing the white dress with pearls, and her white wings were stretched out to her sides.

"And *you* look like trouble," Lazonia said teasingly to Evan. She circled around him and ran her fingers over his slick feathers. "Be careful on your journey home. Do not fly too close to the water. I have a feeling there are a few bull sharks out there who would love to knock you out of the sky."

Aegir interjected, "I will see to it that all of my sea creatures abide by my wishes. None of them shall hurt you."

"Sir, I was wondering about what happened to Dufa?" Evan asked, as he was reminded of the rogue wave.

"She has been dealt with," said Aegir. "You could say she will be grounded for a very long time. No more tsunamis for at least a decade. And on her behalf, I am sorry she tried to drown you."

"Thanks," said Evan, feeling extremely awkward. He then looked at Dr. Irving. "I suppose we should leave the Serpent's Ring with you."

"It must not be kept in Sagaas. It is prudent for you to return the Serpent's Ring home with you," said Dr. Irving.

"But, what will we do with it? Should we return it to your lab?" Evan asked.

"No, that would not be wise. You must find a new place to keep it," added Vor, as she stood next to her hawklike husband.

"How am I supposed to know where to hide it?" said Evan anxiously.

"Dunkle will be there to help. Do not worry. You will know what to do," reassured Dr. Irving.

Lazonia rested her hand on Evan's shoulder. "Evan, you *will* know what to do."

"Lazonia, you really helped. Thanks," said Evan.

"I would do it all again," said Lazonia, and a tear slowly cascaded down her beautiful face.

"Take care," he whispered, wrapping his arms tightly around the mermaid.

"You too," she said, and he loosened his hug.

"Claire, are you ready?" Evan asked.

Claire nodded her head and wiped away a falling tear. She approached Evan, leaving Sigurd behind. She was almost to Evan, when she turned and rushed back to Sigurd, throwing her arms around his neck. Evan was relieved that he couldn't hear what she whispered. With her head hanging down and her hair shielding her face, she eventually joined Evan.

"Goodbye to you all!" announced Evan to the large group of onlookers. "Thanks for seeing us off. And fear not, we will see you again. It's been real." He waved goodbye and turned toward his sister.

"Do you think maybe you overdid that a little? You are such a nerd," she said to him and laughed.

CHAPTER THIRTY

LOOP-THE-LOOPS

D UNKLE AND BARFEL WERE FIRST to take to the air. They flapped their little wings eagerly and did a few loop-the-loops. Evan stretched his long jet-black wings and with a mighty force, brought them down. At once, he shot straight up. He didn't look back to those he had just left. His sinking heart wouldn't allow it.

"How are we supposed to know which way to go? We don't exactly have a map," Evan hollered toward his sister.

"Leave it to me. I know the way," yelled Dunkle, doing another loop.

Evan peered over at Claire. She smiled awkwardly and shrugged. "I guess we follow Dunkle."

"All right, but don't expect me to fly in circles," said Evan.

"Why not? Come on, live a little," said Claire. Surprisingly, she zoomed straight up before diving down toward the sea. Just before touching water, she arched back up, ending her acrobatic stunt in a graceful loop.

"Whoa," said Evan, and his mouth dropped open. "I can't do that."

"Come on, you big wimp. Try it!" she cried out while

197

circling around a few more times.

Evan watched his sister, as she joined the imps in their frolicking. He turned back and noticed the island of Hlesey was a mere speck now. Looking down, he realized they were really high, and in the water below, colorful bull sharks followed along his path. He had a funny feeling they weren't there to give him a friendly send-off.

"Hey guys, we need to move a little faster; we have company," said Evan, pointing toward the sharks.

"Eek, what are they doing?" said Claire, wincing at the sight below. "Aegir said they wouldn't bother us."

"I doubt they're here to say goodbye and thank you. They probably didn't get Aegir's latest message," said Evan.

"Let's go! Let's go!" Barfel yelled and *zip!*—off he raced.

It didn't take long to lose the sharks, and Evan could finally relax and concentrate on flying in a straight, horizontal line. Hours went by like this. After a while, Evan started to wonder if maybe he could have a little fun to pass the time. He added a little more power to his wings and *whoosh!*—he shot straight up before diving toward the ocean. Just before hitting the water, he curved into an arch and finished the loop.

"There you go. How did that feel?" asked Claire.

"Exhilarating, but I won't do it again anytime soon," said Evan, still catching his breath.

"Well, it's good to see you loosen up, little brother," said Claire appraisingly.

Moments later, Barfel announced, "There it is! There it is!"

Evan looked to where the red imp was pointing. Up ahead, the lavender mist gateway came into view. He remembered how on their voyage into Asgard, the mist had shot their boat through the winding tunnel. It was frightening, to say the least. He wondered what it would do to them on their return home.

"When we approach, dive straight into the mist. Hold your wings in tight, and allow it to take you through," advised Dunkle.

"Don't worry, Evan. I'm sure we'll be fine," said Claire. "I'll go through first, okay?"

"Are you sure?" Evan asked, and Claire nodded.

She sped toward the glistening mist, and Evan watched as she increased her speed. Suddenly, she was pulled in and disappeared! Dunkle and Barfel also raced toward the gateway. Then they too were gone.

Evan hesitated briefly and then inched his way toward the looming mist. After taking in a deep breath, he dove. He pulled in his wings, allowing the mist to push him through. To Evan's amazement, his body wasn't rattled by wind. He soared through with relative ease, looping around and through the glass tunnel. In a matter of seconds, he reached the other side.

"See, we made it," said Claire, flying over to him.

"Yeah, we're back," said Evan, looking around. "Hey, wait a minute. The sky is still that strange tangerine color. What's up?"

"You're right; it is," agreed Claire.

"We may have left Asgard, but we're still in Sagaas. Now, we need to hop over to Terra," explained Dunkle, as if it were something you'd say every day.

"How are we going to manage that?" Evan asked.

"Trust me, you will see," said Dunkle, flying toward shore.

Dunkle took the lead, heading in the direction of Greenfield Village. Evan didn't ask; he just followed along, hoping the imp's plan was a good one. At long last, they approached Dr. Irving's house.

"We need to kick-start your world back into motion," said Dunkle, striding toward the front door.

"What does kick-start mean, anyway?" Evan asked, following the determined imp.

Dunkle sighed, "While you were away, time stood still. Now, we need to start it up again." Anxiously, he rushed through the door and into the study.

"Wait a minute! You're telling me that it's still Saturday?" Evan asked and Barfel nodded. Evan tried to understand, but it was just too weird. "But we've been away for almost an entire week."

"Evan, it's probably best if we just roll with it," Claire said and wandered into the study.

The hidden door to the secret room was still open. Last time Evan was here, he had neglected to shut it. Who could blame him? After all, he *was* racing away from what he believed was a security guard. Wow, so much had happened since that day, Evan marveled.

Barfel scurried over to the bookshelf and bounded through the open door. Claire and Evan followed the imps back inside Dr. Irving's secret lab. The room had remained just as Evan had left it. Claire's mess of fallen rubble sat on the floor, untouched. The illustration of Jormundgand was still on the table. And there were still a ton of cobwebs.

"Evan, you need to place the Serpent's Ring over your arm," instructed Dunkle. "Claire, grab onto his arm."

"Just like before," whispered Claire.

"Right, just like before," Dunkle said impatiently. "Evan! Now!"

Evan slid the Serpent's Ring up his arm. His fingertips tingled, and the room took on a warm glow. Claire reached for Evan's arm. He became blinded by white light, and both Claire and Evan were thrown back!

"Sorry, I didn't mean to land on you," said Evan, trying to stand.

"Let's just find Mom and Dad," she said, struggling to her feet.

"Did it work?" Evan asked Dunkle.

"We will have to go outside to know for sure," Dunkle

said as both imps sped toward the front door.

Claire and Evan hurried outside. The sky was now blue instead of tangerine, and from a short distance away the clock tower chimed.

"Claire, we're still wearing the strange-looking clothes we got from Aegir. What are Mom and Dad going to think?" Evan asked.

"Well, Dr. Irving said they won't be able to see them, right, Dunkle?" she asked.

"Only if you would like for them to," reminded Dunkle.

"So, what are they going to see if we don't allow them to see these clothes?" Evan asked.

"Nothing, nothing at all," stated Dunkle.

"Whoa, you mean we won't be wearing anything?" Evan asked.

"That is a good assumption," said Dunkle.

"Won't they see us in the clothes we were wearing before all of this?" Claire asked.

"Why would they? You left those behind," said Dunkle.

"Great," said Claire. "So, it's either we're without clothes or wearing these?"

"Correct," said Dunkle.

"Why can't you just change what they look like?" Evan asked.

"Why bother? They'll still look different from what we were wearing this morning. Besides, I like this dress. I wouldn't mind keeping it for the Homecoming Dance."

"All right, fine. I won't see anyone I know here, anyway. I don't want to lie to Mom and Dad, but we'll have to come up with a good reason for wearing these," said Evan. "We should probably lose the wings. Don't you think? They're cool and all, but a little impractical."

"I have grown rather fond of *my* wings," said Dunkle. "I would like to keep them, if you do not mind."

"Me too! Me too!" announced Barfel.

"Right, leave that one to me," Claire said and removed

201

Evan's wings and then her own.

"So, I guess this is goodbye," Evan said to Dunkle and Barfel. "I suppose Claire and I should hide the Serpent's Ring?"

"No, we can manage," said Dunkle. "You have helped enough, already."

"Well then, here it is. Guard it well."

"I shall," said Dunkle, now clutching the golden ring. He stared down. "I will miss you Evan and Claire Jones."

"Me too! Me too!" chimed Barfel.

"We can come and visit you," said Evan.

"Sure, we'll come back next weekend," said Claire, lifting up Dunkle and hugging him tight.

With that, Barfel leapt into the arms of an unprepared Evan, who was slightly taken aback.

"I'll miss you too," Evan said and quickly placed him down.

Dunkle rushed to Evan and wrapped his arms around Evan's legs. Evan lifted him and gave him a big squeeze.

"This isn't goodbye. I'll see you very soon," Evan reassured the sobbing imp.

Claire and Evan backed away. Dunkle and Barfel waved and then slowly faded. They simply vanished.

"I didn't know they could disappear," said Evan. "The crazy thing is that I think I will really miss those guys."

"I will too, but I really want to see Mom and Dad," said Claire. "It's time to run!"

They hurried over to the clock tower, where their parents were waiting for them.

"Look, there they are," announced Evan, feeling a rush of relief.

CHAPTER THIRTY-ONE

UNINVITED GUESTS

J UST AS EVAN WAS CLOSE enough to reach out and touch his mom, she turned. Her eyes narrowed and she asked, "Where have you two been?"

Evan didn't respond, he simply ran around the bench and hugged her.

"Mom, Dad!" declared Evan, still embracing his Mom.

"This is unexpected. Nice, but unexpected," said Mom.

"I'm not going to miss out on a rare hug from my son," said Dad, joining them, too.

"It's so good to see you," said Claire, wedging her way into the family hug.

Their parents relaxed their posture, and Evan released them.

"We have so much to tell you," Evan began, but was nudged by Claire.

"Where did you two find those clothes?" Mom asked.

"We have a great explanation for how we came by them," stated Claire.

"Yeah, tell them Claire," said Evan, not wanting to fabricate a story. After all, he was never very good at lying.

"Well, we stumbled upon a theatre group. The director needed two people to fill in for some sick actors. We volunteered," Claire said sort of convincingly.

"Now, that's the spirit," said Dad enthusiastically. "When do we get to see the play?"

"It's over," snapped Evan.

"That's a shame. Well, we had better return those gorgeous costumes," said Mom, admiring the pearls on Claire's dress.

"That's not necessary. They, um, gave them to us," said Claire.

"Yeah, as payment for helping out," interceded Evan.

Claire and Evan's parents looked at each other quizzically. Evan's palms were sweaty. Roughly and urgently, he wiped them over his white tunic and baggy pants.

After a long, torturing silence, their Dad said, "Well, you missed the clock tower. What do you want to see next?"

"We're game for whatever. Right, Evan?" said Claire, staring at her brother expectantly.

"Yeah, we'll go wherever you want," agreed Evan.

"It's getting a little hot outside. Why don't we head indoors," Dad said and started to walk. "Ah, if only each item could speak. They'd have quite a fascinating story to tell. Did you know a room from the very first Holiday Inn is sitting inside, right now? And next to that is the very first ..."

Dad continued with his historical dissertation about many of the artifacts they would soon get to see. This time, Evan tried to pay closer attention and discovered it was sort of interesting after all.

A couple of days later, life had returned to normal—a

very calm, nice normal. Evan no longer dreamt of colorful stingrays and terrifying bull sharks. In fact, each morning he struggled, trying to remember his dreams but couldn't. As was typical on weekdays, his parents returned to work. And since Claire and Evan were still on summer vacation, they were left on their own.

Claire spent much of her time staring into her golden locket. Sometimes, she spoke with Sigurd. Sometimes, she simply viewed the world they had just left. One day, Evan overheard her speaking with Vor, asking all sorts of questions.

Evan had returned to playing video games and watching TV. But it felt less satisfying than it had before. Surprisingly, he was restless, anxious to go on another adventure. And although he and Claire got along much better after their quest, they barely spoke. Whenever they were alone, he desperately wanted to rehash events from their journey. But all he had to do was look at Claire's saddened face and know some things were better left unsaid.

It was on a Thursday morning when he felt enough time had passed to approach his sister. Even if she didn't care to, he needed to talk about what had happened.

He found her in the kitchen, eating a bowl of cereal.

"Claire, can we talk about Sagaas?" he asked.

"Sure," she said, and he joined her at the table.

"Vor said we would return one day," started Evan. "Has she given you any more information?"

"No, she won't reveal information about the future. All she says is that in time, events will unfold. You're just going to have to hang tight."

"Right," Evan sighed. "Hey, do you think Dad will take us back to Greenfield Village this weekend? I'd really like to see Dunkle and Barfel."

Without warning—POP!—Dunkle and Barfel arrived in Evan's kitchen. The entire area instantly smelled like pine and cedar. Evan inhaled the woodland scent and smiled.

"What are you doing here?" Claire asked, also grinning.

"Did you not call? I distinctly believe I heard my name," said Dunkle.

"You did! You did!" cheered Barfel.

"Wait a minute. You can come to us when we say your name?" Evan asked. "You failed to mention that before."

"Hum, I am mentioning it to you now," said Dunkle. "Besides, we are not able to teleport in Sagaas, only in your world."

"It's good to see you both," said Claire, smiling more than she had in days.

"So, where did you hide the Serpent's Ring?" Evan asked curiously. He had been wondering about its whereabouts for days now.

Dunkle and Barfel looked sheepishly at each other, and then Dunkle approached Evan. He removed the Serpent's Ring from behind his back and offered it to him.

"You haven't hidden it yet?" Evan asked anxiously.

"In a word, no," said Dunkle.

"We tried! We tried!" exclaimed Barfel.

"We have tried, but we have not been able to find a suitable location," said Dunkle.

"We could hide the Serpent's Ring here," interjected Claire.

"It can't stay here! Have you lost your mind?" yelled Evan.

"And you guys could stay in the basement," rationalized Claire. "Mom and Dad never go down there. This way, we can help protect the Serpent's Ring. Besides, Evan, the only way to return to Sagaas is to open a portal. We'll need to have access to the Serpent's

Ring if we want to go back."

"Yippee! Yippee!" Barfel hollered and danced around the kitchen, leaping onto the center island and twirling.

"Dunkle, if you stay here, Barfel can't do that in the main part of the house," said Evan. "In fact, you'll have to stay down in the basement."

"Your parents will not be able to see us," said Dunkle.

"Right, but they will be able to see the mess Barfel makes," Evan said and cringed. Barfel had just knocked down some lids from a hanging pot-rack with his wings.

"Good point," said Dunkle.

"Come on. Let's go to the basement," said Evan. "We need to find a good hiding spot for the Serpent's Ring."

"And help our guests settle in. Dunkle, Barfel, right this way," Claire said politely and led them to the stairs.

Her foot hadn't reached the bottom step before Dunkle and Barfel had nudged her aside and were running around the basement. Evan flicked on the light and watched the two imps explore. Unfortunately, they wanted to explore every single thing within view, and some things that were not.

"Remember, you shouldn't have to go upstairs for anything," said Evan. "Claire and I will bring you food. There's a bathroom right over there, where you'll find a nice shower and scented soap. Please feel free to use a lot of it. And try not to make it too obvious that you guys are living down here. You know, just in case Mom or Dad do come down here."

"Evan, relax," reassured Claire. "The imps will be fine. Come on, we need to find a good hiding place."

Evan leaned closer to Claire and said in a hushed tone, "All right, but I have a funny feeling our lives will never be the same."

THE END

Coming Soon

Relics of Mysticus:

Book Two

The Trickster's Totem

Magical Food Recipes

POPPIN-DROPPIN CHOCOLATE CRÈME CENTER

2 eggs
1/3 cup granulated sugar
2 tablespoons cornstarch
1 cup semi-sweet chocolate morsels
3/4 cup milk
1 tablespoon cold water
1 teaspoon sweet-cream butter, softened
1/2 cup heavy cream, whipped
2 tablespoons chocolate truffle guffle (for purpose of multiplication)*

1. Use a whisk to beat eggs in a medium bowl. Now, spin around the floor 6 times.

2. Stir the granulated sugar, cornstarch, semi-sweet chocolate morsels, and chocolate truffle guffle in a saucepan.

3. Add milk and stir until the mixture is smooth.

4. Cook and stir over medium heat, until mixture boils and thickens. Chant, "Poppin-Droppin, Poppin-Droppin".

5. Remove saucepan from heat. Gradually stir half the milk into the eggs.

6. Return egg mixture to saucepan. Cook and stir over medium heat for 1 minute.

7. Remove saucepan from heat and place on a hot pad.

8. It is imperative at this point that you drop to the floor and hop like a frog. Repeat 5 times.

9. Fold the whipped cream into chocolate cream. Cover and refrigerate the cream mixture for 15 minutes or until well chilled. Clap, clap, clap.

PUFFED PASTRY FOR THE POPPIN-DROPPIN

1 cup water
1/2 cup sweet-cream butter
1 cup sifted flour
1/4 teaspoon salt
4 eggs
2 tablespoons pink pixie crystals (for purpose of bouncing)*

1. Pre-heat oven to 400 F. In a saucepan, heat water and butter to a rolling boil.
2. Stir in flour, pink pixie crystals and salt. Continue to stir vigorously over low heat, until mixture leaves the pan and forms into a ball (about 1 minute).
3. Remove from heat. Chant, "Puffin, puffin, puffin! Up!"
4. Thoroughly, beat in 1 egg at a time. Stir until smooth. Drop batter onto an ungreased baking sheet into tablespoon sized balls. Twirl, twirl, twirl, twirl.
5. Bake at 400 F for 45 minutes. Allow to cool slowly.

Using a fiddle-tube (or traditional pastry tube, if necessary), fill inside of each pastry with chocolate crème. Sprinkle top with confectioners' sugar. Enjoy!

*In the event you do not have access to ingredients that are magical in nature (chocolate truffle guffle and pink pixie crystals), if omitted the flavor will not be affected; however, the Poppin-Droppin might lose its ability to multiply and bounce.

WOOFOUT BAR

1/4 cup all-purpose flour
1/2 cup butter-flavored shortening
1/3 cup white sugar
3/4 cup raspberry preserves
1/2 cup raisins
1/2 cup milk chocolate chips
1/4 cup honey
2 tablespoons butter
3/4 cup quick-cooking oats
1/3 cup shredded coconut
1/3 cup sliced almonds
2 tablespoons sesame seeds
2 tablespoons ground bark from dawgbark tree (Caution: might cause temporary reaction in humans)*

1. Preheat oven to 350 F degrees. Grease one 9x9 inch square pan.

2. In a mixing bowl, combine the flour, ground dawgbark, shortening, and sugar. Beat at low speed until crumbly. Use a proper bapple-doodle (or a traditional spatula, if necessary) to press mixture into the bottom of the prepared pan.

3. Bake at 350 F for 15 to 20 minutes. Chant, "Whoof-arrough-uff" 3 times.

4. Combine preserves, raisins, and chocolate pieces. Stir until blended. Set aside.

5. In a saucepan, combine the honey and butter. Cook and stir until melted (be careful not to boil). Stir in the oats, coconuts, almonds, and sesame seeds until blended.

6. Spread the raspberry preserve mixture over the hot crust. Spoon oat mixture on top, spreading evenly to edges of pan. Bake for an additional 15 to 20 minutes or until lightly browned. Cut into bars to serve.

*In the event you do not have access to ingredients magical in nature (dawgbark tree), it will not affect the flavor; however, it might lose its ability to cause a human to bark like a dog.

FIZZY WHIZZLE

1 pinch pixie powder (be very careful when handling)*
1 gallon ginger pop

1.Pour ginger pop into glass pitcher.
2.Very carefully, and I stress carefully, sprinkle one pinch of pixie powder into each individual glass.
3.Pour ginger pop over Round Raspberry Ice.

*In the event you do not have access to ingredients magical in nature (pixie powder), it will not affect the flavor; however, it might lose its ability to change color. Candy Pixie Sticks may be substituted if necessary.

ROUND RASPBERRY ICE

1 ice-cube tray with round impressions
fresh water
raspberries

1. Pour water into tray.
2. Drop one raspberry into each round impressions.
3. Freeze for a few hours or until solid.
4. Add to glass of Fizzy Whizzle.

*This works well with lemon slices, too.

REFERENCE

Aegir is the Norse god of the sea.

Asgard is the home of the Norse gods.

Bergkonge is a mythical creature with scaly skin, wings, and a long tail. He breathes fire and wears an armor of bones. His name translates to "Mountain King." He is known to seduce women who travel alone in the forest and then brings them to the mountain. These women are never heard from again. The Mountain King is described as a handsome man, covered in a cape made of leaves.

Draugr possess superhuman strength, can increase their size at will, and carry the unmistakable stench of decay. They are undead Vikings that retain some semblance of intelligence, and who delight in the suffering that they cause. Draugar is Draugr in its plural form.

Fairy is a supernatural being, usually resembling a small person, with magic powers. Fairies could be either kindly or malicious.

Giants are hideous with deformed features, with little brainpower.

Hawk is a bird of prey that is active in the daytime, normally having broad wings, a short hooked beak, strong talons, and a long tail.

Hlesey is an island above the Undersea Hall of Aegir and Ran.

Huldra is from Norse mythology, a woman with long blond hair who always wears a crown made of flowers. She has the tail of a cow. She is believed to seduce young unmarried men into marrying her. If he agrees, then she will change into an ugly woman with the strength of ten men and lose her tail.

Imps are often small and not very attractive creatures. They are seen only by the most observant people because they like to hide. They have been known to be wild and uncontrollable. Often taking jokes too far, they tend to irritate most humans. Imps have also been known as being "bound" to some sort of object. In the case of Dunkle, he is attached to the Serpent's Ring and is sworn to protect it.

Jormundgand is a serpent so enormous that he is able to wrap himself around the world. If he were to let go, the world would end.

Jotunheim is the land of giants in Norse mythology.

Labyrinth is a place with a lot of complicated passages, tunnels, or paths in which it would be easy to become lost.

Mermaid is a mythical sea creature with the head and upper body of a woman and the tail of a fish instead of legs.

Mysticus Latin for mysterious or enigma.

Odin is the king of the Norse gods, god of poetry, battle and death He is a very important god.

Ran is married to Aegir and was known to drown men in her net and pull them under.

Sea Serpent is a giant snake often reported to have been seen at sea.

Serpent's Ring is transmuted gold, shaped like Jormundgand (a serpent forming a circle with its body and biting its tail). In this tale only, the Serpent's Ring is a key to unlocking Jormundgand.

Sigurd is a mythological hero in Norse mythology.

He killed Fafnir, who was in dragon form, and bathed in Fafnir's blood thus becoming immortal.

Telekinetic is the mental power to move objects without the use of physical force.

Terra is Latin for Earth.

Transfiguration is to have the ability to transform the appearance of something or somebody.

Trolls are fearsome members of the Scandinavian society who live in the wilderness or in caves. They are devious beings with oversize ears and noses.

The Undersea Hall holds Aegir and Ran's grand festivals to both gods and mortals, in Norse mythology.

Vor is the goddess who knows it all.

The Waves are the nine daughters of Aegir and Ran. Each of their names has a different meaning.

Himinglaeva is a reference to the transparency of water and that through which one can see the heavens.

Dufa is the pitching or plunging one.

Blooughadda is a reference to red sea foam.

Hefring is the riser.

Uor is frothing wave.

Hronn is welling wave.

Bylgja is billow.

Drofn is foam-fleck.

Kolga is cool wave.

Many believe Norse gods and other mythological beings of ancient Scandinavia represent aspects of the personalities, our emotions and many qualities that make up the psyche of the human self.

The Serpent's Ring is loosely based on Norse myth.

ABOUT THE AUTHOR

Currently, H.B. Bolton resides in sunny Florida with her supportive husband, two adorable children, gorgeous greyhounds, and scruffy mutt. She is actively creating new worlds and interesting characters for the next book in one of her series. Shhhh, can you keep a secret? Not only does she write books for the young-at-heart, adventurous sort who yearn to dive into a good young-adult fantasy story, she also writes spellbinding, heart pounding women's fiction. These particular books are written under the name Barbara Brooke, but that's another story, altogether.

Check out her websites
http://www.hbbolton.com
http://www.barbarabrookeglimmers.com

Become a fan on facebook
http://www.facebook.com/HBBoltonAuthor
http://facebook.com/#!/BarbaraBrookeAuthor

Find her on Twitter
https://twitter.com/#!/H_B_Bolton
https://twitter.com/#!/Barbara_Brooke

Barbara Brooke has a blog
http://www.barbarabrooke.wordpress.com

Acknowledgments

Thank you to all of those who have helped and supported me in making this novel a reality: Erica Michael's for spending countless hours nurturing both me and my manuscript; Elisabeth Alba for designing and illustrating an amazing book cover; the team over at Streetlight Graphics for adding a touch of professionalism to the overall appearance of my novels; and to Cindy Martin for swooping in to help save the day.

Made in the USA
Lexington, KY
05 August 2012